Marie Bradby

some friend

SCHOLASTIC INC.

New York Toronto London Auckland Sydney
Mexico City New Delhi Hong Kong Buenos Aires

ISBN-13: 978-0-545-04454-7
ISBN-10: 0-545-04454-5

12 11 10 9 8 7 6 5 4 3 2   8 9 10 11/0

Printed in the U.S.A.   40
First Scholastic printing, September 2007
The text for this book is set in Lomba.

For my sisters Joyce and Deborah;
my writing sisters Ann, George Ella, Jan, Leatha,
Lou, and Martha; and my found sisters Claudia,
Cynthia, Deane, Fabienne, Judith, Lydia, and Sanae.
You are fabulous friends!

some
friend

1

CHUM

All my life I've been hoping I'd find a friend so I wouldn't have to play Monopoly by myself. (When I get the box out and set up all the little bitty houses and the fake money, everybody in my family suddenly gets too busy and just disappears.) If I had a friend, I'd have somebody to walk to the grocery store with when Mama forgets the one thing that she went for. We could sing songs and do the latest dance steps—the pony, the Watusi, and the twist—and, you know, just hang out.

She would be my best friend, and I would ask her questions about the three-letter word—"b-r-a." I am in training, though I don't know for what. My bra leaves ridges on my rib cage and they itch. I usually rush right home from school and take it off.

There. Whew!

Better get downstairs and start my homework. It's always best to look busy. When you're not doing your homework, people ask you things like: "Can you take these smelly vegetable peelings out to the compost?"

I sit at the dining-room table and put my name and the date on a sheet of loose-leaf paper. *Pearl Jordan. Wednesday, March 6, 1963.* I don't know why, but I add: *Mrs. Scott. Fifth Grade.* Then I start diagramming sentences and wonder what kind of job anyone would need this for.

IGNORED

Sometimes I feel so big—full of ideas about things, like stuff right here in my backyard in Fairfax, Virginia. I think I am going to be a scientist because there are so many questions that we need to figure out. I mean, somebody has to worry about what's important.

For instance, in winter, when my head just about snaps off from shivering while I wait at the school bus stop, I wonder: *How do the squirrels in our tree keep from freezing in their nests?* In summer I look at hummingbirds and wonder: *Do they get tired of beating their wings fifty times a second?* And I wonder why—when it's hot as blazes outside—worms pick that particular time to crawl out of some safe, cozy hole in the grass and get fried on the sidewalk.

Other things too. What holds airplanes up? The only time I have flown was last year, when my fourth-grade class went to New York City for the day to see the Empire State Building and the Statue of Liberty. We all piled into this great big airplane, the propellers got to whirling around, and after racing down the runway, it just rose off the ground. How do they do that? Something so enormous and heavy. And how do those pilots know where to go? Do they have a map of the clouds?

If I had a friend, we could talk this over and maybe figure it out. Maybe even win an award—like at the school science fair.

Or I could tell her something that I *have* figured out: People don't notice what you want them to notice, but they sure have X-ray eyes when you don't want them to see what you are doing!

"Mama, I grew a foot last week," I announced yesterday.

"That's nice, sweetie," she said, not even looking up from the bookkeeping work she does at the kitchen table for her part-time job.

You see what I mean?

"But I need some new jeans," I said. "The bottoms of these are up to my knees."

"Mmm-hmm . . ."

Then this morning there is no juice because I'm the last one in the bathroom (shared by Mama, Daddy, my older sister Diana, my big brother Curtis, and my baby sister Angela) and the last one to get breakfast, so I am dying of thirst, and out of desperation, I pop open an orange soda, and Mama's head zips around like a robot in a TV show.

"Just what do you think you're doing?"

"But I was—"

"Young lady, sodas are not for breakfast!"

"But I was just—"

"Don't 'but' me. Do you want rotten teeth? Or worse, stomach cancer?"

"I was thirsty."

"That's what they make water for. And as I have just paid the water bill, there's plenty of it. Do you hear me?"

"Yes, ma'am."

FAMILY FEET

My mother has the prettiest feet. They are small and dainty. With cute little toes. While I am diagramming sentences, I sneak a peek at them under the kitchen table, her shoes kicked off. On Saturday afternoons, after we have finished cleaning house all morning, Mama takes a bath and gives herself a pedicure. She cuts, files, and paints her toenails. She puts on her open-toed shoes and sits on the front porch with her crossword puzzle magazines and her lemonade and waves at people passing by. When Daddy finishes chores and errands, they go walking after dinner—to the park, to the shopping center—to show the world feet that would make Cinderella jealous.

A friend would help you with a pedicure. She wouldn't laugh at your feet, even if your toenail was blue and falling off.

Angela has sweaty feet. They are hot and fat, and she's always putting them on me when we sleep together at Auntie Gert's. Then we end up in a fight, but does Auntie Gert make Angela keep her porky little hooves on her side of the bed? No. She makes me sleep on the divan. Maybe this is really what I want anyway. It's cozy on that divan; the pillows are so fluffy, I just sink right into them. And it's right beside the end table where there is a picture of me and Auntie Gert, and we are wearing matching sunglasses and having so much fun—just the two of us.

No one has ever seen Diana's feet. At home Diana is covered from head to toe in towels, sweatpants, bathrobes, socks, and slippers. Prissy missy. But the minute she hits that door, boy, it's show time. Blouse unbuttoned to here, the sheerest stockings she can find. Mama does not know this, but as soon as Diana rounds the street corner and meets her friends, she rolls the top of her skirt over to hitch it up and show her knees.

Curtis's feet just plain stink. If he leaves his tennis shoes in the kitchen, they'll smell up the whole room. And are they huge! They look like hams. And his feet are still growing.

"Cut the toes out," Daddy told him from behind the newspaper the other day. "That's what I do for my bunions."

"What?" Curtis asked, resting a basketball on his hip.

"Make a slit on the side of the shoe to give your feet some room," Daddy said. When Curtis scrunched up his face, Daddy put down the newspaper and asked, "Didn't I just buy you some new tennis shoes?"

"Yes, sir, but that was back in September. . . . I need new ones."

"Son, I am not made of money. When I was growing up, we made our own shoes and—"

"Was that when you had to walk five miles in the snow to go to school?"

"What?"

"Nothing."

Of course, then Curtis just asks Mama, and she "sugar babys" him and buys him Converse Chuck Taylor All Stars—top-of-the-line sneakers.

Me, there is nothing special about my feet. About the only thing you used to be able to say was that they were skinny, like the rest of me. But one day Curtis changed all that when we were playing "Throw the Boulder as Far as You Can," and he heaved one that was bigger than Mama's purse and it went sideways and landed right on my left foot. Ye-owwww! It hurt worse than the time I fell off of my bike in Lenore's gravel driveway. The doctor said that I was lucky it wasn't broken. Lucky? My big toe swelled up, turned red, then purple, then black. Then the toenail fell off.

STUCK

Sometimes I feel small. Like I am that tiny little bump that's left after the leaf falls from the tree. That's because even in a crowded house, I'm still mostly by myself. Just little me. But I am not small.

If I jump, I can reach the basketball net. If Mama paid more attention to me, she'd see that I am not a baby like Angela. I don't need a sitter after school when Mama has to deliver her paperwork for her bookkeeping job. And she doesn't have to read to me at night when she reads to "Little Miss Angel." I have been reading novels since I was in the second grade, thank you. It's like Mama hasn't noticed. I'll be married and she'll come over to my house and still want to read to me. It will be *so* embarrassing.

M A P

I know my street by heart. Every pothole, every dog barking behind a chain-link fence, every cherry tree waiting to be climbed. Every car that sits all week until Sunday morning. Past Nadine Dawson's house. Her grandfather's brand-new 1963 Cadillac gleaming in the sun. Past pesky Dink's. Past Miss Lela's, roses still rising up the side of her house and blooming sometimes in December. She's got the prettiest roses around.

Nadine. She'd be fun, I guess. Except she's not the best speller. Caused our group at school to lose the spelling contest. Anyhow, farther down the street, there is the corner and the stoplight and the playground. Another light. The gas station, the grocery store, and the shopping center.

That's if I go straight there. If I go left down the second side street, I will come to Lenore's. Everybody wants to be her friend. Her house is pretty much like mine, except she doesn't have any brothers or sisters, and she has a room all to herself with things I can only dream of.

There are three of us girls in "my" room. Princess Diana has her very own desk and her very own bed with a bedspread that Grandma made her just before she died. Diana never has to share anything. I sleep in a double bed with Angela. Yep, a saggy old bed that if you sit on it wrong, the mattress will collapse onto the floor because the slats sometimes slip out of place.

Though it's out of the way, I always go down Lenore's street, as if it's as natural as pie to make a little circle when I'm going to the grocery. Lenore's sort of my friend. Well, she would be if Mama would let me wear nylon stockings instead of kneesocks.

HAG

Then there is Mrs. Mumby. She lives near the playground in a creepy old house with a front porch so stacked with boxes and stuff that it looks like she's always having a rummage sale. I don't think she ever had a friend. She's too old and shriveled like a witch and yells at kids from her front porch. She has a hump in her back and doesn't stand up straight. *And* she has a wart on her nose. Well, I just made that up 'cause she's a snitch. I mean, was she the same but only smaller when she was a girl? I don't know.

CHUMP

Finding a friend isn't easy. There aren't too many kids here around my age, which is eleven. Besides, you can find girls to be your friends and then find out that they are not. And sometimes your friends do dumb stuff—that doesn't mean that you have to do it too. But if I did, before I hit the door, some nosy body (do I need to tell you who?) would have already told my mama, and she would be waiting to catch me like a rabbit in a trap.

BROCCOLI

Trees. That's what I call them. That's about how interesting they taste, too. After school a week later, I am searching the bin of vegetables at Swan's Market. We're having meatloaf for dinner, and Mama has run out of vegetables to go with it.

There are things in this store that I would not touch. Brussels sprouts for one. And turnips. Who likes turnips, really?

I pull up the collar on my jacket. It's always cold in the grocery store, with all these big coolers blowing cold air.

"What're you looking for?" the manager asks. That's Mr. Norton. He is a beady-eyed man with pale, stringy hair that he has plastered to his scalp with Vitalis. He is unloading cartons of vegetables.

"My mother wants broccoli."

"Got some over there. On sale."

I know Mama hates it when I spend too much for something, so I go on over. Hmm, twenty cents. Limp as a dishrag, though. Stalks turning gray, the little buds are turning yellow. A blond-haired woman comes up looking for the same thing. Mr. Norton shows her a fresh carton that he is just

11

opening. She oohs and aahs. As I watch him put some broccoli in a paper bag for her, I rub the three quarters that I have in my pocket and weave them through my fingers. I still have to get mayonnaise for tomorrow's lunch sandwiches. There will be enough change for me to get a Brown Cow sucker if I get a bunch of broccoli from the sale table. I'm not going to eat it anyway.

I put a few stalks of the sale broccoli in a paper sack and run over to the baking aisle and grab a large jar of Duke's mayonnaise. Then I head to the checkout counter and pore over the five-cent candy. Jujubees, Good & Plenty, Squirrel Nuts, Baby Ruths, Fifth Avenues. Ahh, a Brown Cow! Last one. I grab it.

I'm not sure that I can afford it, though. "Can you ring this first and give me a subtotal?" I ask the pimply-faced kid at the checkout.

"You only have three things," he says, glaring.

"So?"

He rolls his eyes and weighs the broccoli, then rings it up with the mayonnaise. "So far that's seventy cents," he says, folding his arms across his chest.

Great! I think. I hand him the sucker and the

three quarters. Then I snatch the sucker back. Oh, shoot. Tax! "Is there tax?"

"Yep. The new sales tax. That'll be seventy-two cents."

I keep staring at him while I search all my pockets—my two front pockets, my two back pockets, my two coat pockets, the tiny coin pocket on my jeans. While I am doing this, I notice that two of them have holes.

A line builds behind me.

"Come on!" the checker snarls. I look sideways. A woman behind me clears her throat. A man taps his foot.

"Look, I don't have all day!" the boy says.

Then I have an idea. "Could you just put back a small piece of the broccoli?"

"Oh, geez, come on!" the foot-tapping man says, looking at his watch.

The clerk grabs the bag, takes out a piece of the limp, yellowed broccoli, and shoves the bag at me. "Get out of here!" he says.

"But I need a receipt."

He rips off the receipt, whips it out toward me, and tosses me one green S&H coupon stamp. I snatch them and run out of the store.

A block away I sit down on the bus bench and peel the paper off my Brown Cow and start licking away. When the candy is half gone and my tongue is all bumpy from licking the dark chocolate, my stomach starts to feel queasy. If I eat any more, I'll get sick. I rewrap it and save the rest for later. Better get back.

I walk down the street, passing buses of people coming home from work, row after row of houses, yards, fences, then I come to the park. A bunch of kids are playing a "mean" game of basketball. I really should go straight on home. Oh, there's a bright blue jacket with a large yellow hornet on it. It's Curtis. He's playing with the others. Though Mama is waiting, I run on over.

2

HAMMERED

Lots of older girls sit on the bench and watch the boys play. They don't really look at the boys. They file their nails or braid each other's hair or just pop chewing gum and sing.

I stand on the side and watch Curtis and the other boys run up and down the court. Though the boys are probably smelly because they are drenched in sweat, I wish I could play.

The ball rolls out-of-bounds toward me and I scoop it up, nearly running into a kid, and toss it back to Valentine. All the girls think he's cute. I can't imagine what all the fuss is about. Looks just like another boy to me.

"Thanks," he says.

Curtis's team—in the white undershirts—is playing hard, but they are down by about ten points.

I motion to Curtis, mouthing: "Can I play?" and he scrunches up his face and waves me off.

The ball rolls my way again and I toss it to him. "Aren't you supposed to be at Swan's?" he asks.

"I went," I answer, ignoring what he really means.

On the next drive, Curtis bounce-passes the ball to one of his teammates, and two guards clobber the boy. He crumples to the concrete, holding his knee.

The bench girls turn around and make ticking sounds with their teeth. "Aww, see there! You have gone and hurt Melon," one says.

Curtis helps Melon to the bench and the girls move back a bit.

"You gonna call it quits?" Valentine asks Curtis, bouncing the ball.

"Can't you see he's hurt?" Curtis says. "We're short now."

"You were short before that," Valentine says, laughing.

"Aww, he's ranking on you," another girl says.

I move over to Curtis and set the bag on the bench. "I'll play," I say. He doesn't pay me any mind.

Valentine and his boys keep shooting, and this time when the ball rolls my way, I start bouncing it and move onto the court and shoot. *Swish.*

"You should have picked your little sister," Valentine says. "She's good."

I blush. The guys start shooting again and I stay on the court. When the ball comes my way again, I dribble and fake and put one up. *Swish.*

"All right!" Valentine yells.

You learn about driving and shooting when you are alone and you have finished your homework and done the dishes and picked up your room and folded your clothes and drawn hundreds of pictures of birds or trees or hands that don't look like birds or trees or hands—though you are certain you are supposed to be an artist. Even though it's just you and the ball against the garage door, you know that hundreds, no, thousands of people are watching and cheering your every move. . . . And I can feel it, eyes watching me when it's my turn to do my moves and shoot. And though the sun is weak on the horizon, it's as if that yellow spotlight is shining just on me. All the air around me seems yellow and bright.

The ball rolls out-of-bounds, and this girl standing by herself on the other side of the court picks it up. Even she looks yellow. But instead of tossing it back to Marcus, who has run after it, she bounce-passes it to me.

"You nappy-headed Zulu!" he says to her. A bunch of people crack up while I swerve and dip

17

and go for a layup, but Marcus cuts me off and I land right on my butt. Everybody laughs. But the pain in my tailbone is sharp enough to make me cry. I fight back tears.

Marcus holds the ball on his hip and says, "What is this, man? Are we going to play, or are we going to be fooling with some stupid girl?"

"I am not stupid!" I yell, and try to get up, but the pain is worse, deep in my bones.

"Okay, okay," Valentine says. "I was just having some fun. Now, little girl, you go on back to your doll babies." Everybody laughs again. The bench girls slap their thighs.

"I don't have any doll babies," I say. But they are still laughing and start to play right over the top of me.

I feel myself being lifted up under my arms. It's Curtis. He guides me to the side.

"Come on," he says.

"But—"

"Get your stuff and come on." He puts his towel around his neck and starts walking off.

"Later, man," he hollers over his shoulder. "I'll catch you on the rebound."

I grab the bag and hurry to catch up to Curtis. Then I remember the girl and turn to wave at her, but she is gone. Maybe there was no girl in the first place. I follow behind my brother. "I can outshoot all of them," I say.

"Pearl, they weren't really playing you hard."

"But I can too play."

Curtis stops and looks back at me. "Pearl, they don't want to play with girls."

"Humph. Well, I don't want to play with them!" I stomp my foot, but that hurts my butt. I think boys don't want to play with girls who are better than them.

I wash up and set the dining-room table—forks on the left, knives on the right. Angela is supposed to help. She is supposed to give everyone a napkin. Fat chance. She is busy with her Chatty Cathy doll, pulling the string that makes her talk and pretending that the doll is a movie star. Chubby, fat-cheeked, baby-faced, pigeon-toed Chatty. Even though she has blond curls and blue eyes, she would not make a good beauty-pageant contestant.

I go back in the kitchen to get water glasses, and I see Mama staring at the broccoli that she has just dumped out of the bag with the green stamp.

"What is this mess?" she says.

Mama doesn't say anything about the broccoli during dinner. She talks to Daddy about cleaning up the yard now that spring is coming and getting seeds started for the garden. She tells him that she saw a clematis shoot at the hardware store that would look nice on the trellis in the backyard.

No, she doesn't even mention broccoli. Instead, we eat Brussels sprouts, frozen from last summer. "Mmm, good," Daddy says, plopping a whole one in his mouth. "Reminds me of my granddaddy's place."

The rest of us can hardly swallow. I take the smallest bite possible. I get one sprout down in bits and pieces. *Two to go,* I think, then notice that I still have three.

There is a grin spreading across Curtis's face as wide as the Potomac River. "May I be excused?" he asks. "I have a lot of homework."

"Yes, you may," Daddy answers, and I am stuck.

After dinner Mama tells Diana to clean up. I am pleased to hear that order until Mama says, "And *you* are coming with me."

"What'd I do?" I ask, feeling guilty and wishing instead that I were scraping dishes or scrubbing pots.

"We're going to the store. Get your jacket." Mama puts on her camel-hair coat and her high heels, and we head out.

The days are longer now that it's mid-March. The sun is still up as we walk to the grocery store. Mama holds my hand as we cross at the lights. She hasn't done this in a long time. Since Angela was born. Since she finished college at night and got that bookkeeping job.

I love the feel of her coat—so silky soft. I hug her arm and let the furry cloth caress my cheek. "You look beautiful, Mom," I say.

"Why, thank you, sugar."

"I wish I had a coat like this."

"You'll have a coat like this one day. Remember how long I waited for this coat?"

I nod my head.

"I had it on layaway forever. Winter was past before I paid it off. A person might not have all the best clothes, but one nice coat makes up for that. When you have a nice coat, you don't have to have expensive clothes underneath.

"My mother had a saying: 'Always buy the best that you can afford—even if you can only buy one.'"

Inside the store Mama spots slick-headed Mr. Norton right away. "Good evening," he says. "What can I do for you?"

"I had a taste for broccoli," Mama says.

"Your girl got some earlier, didn't she?"

My mother puts her manicured finger to her cheek. "That was broccoli?"

Mr. Norton looks puzzled. "I sent her to the table right over there where the sale vegetables are."

My mother looks around. "Oh, that *used* to be broccoli. You know, when my vegetables are gone by like that, I put them on the compost heap."

Mr. Norton narrows his eyes. "Well, Miss . . . Miss . . ."

"Mrs. Jordan," Mama says.

"Mrs. Jordan, I just got a crate of regular-priced broccoli," he says, pointing.

Mama looks over the contents of the crate and feels a few pieces. "What else did you get?" she asks.

"Asparagus, but it's expensive."

"Really?" she asks, looking around. "I see you have artichokes, too. . . . And avocados."

"They're really good. I carry them for my best customers."

"Is that right?"

"Uh-huh."

"Well, I'll take an avocado *and* some asparagus."

Mr. Norton scrunches up his face and puts the vegetables in paper bags. "Is that all?" he asks.

"You know, I think I'll also take an artichoke."

"Okay." He puts that in a bag too. "Your little girl is the one who picked out the broccoli, not me," he adds. "I'll tell you what, I've got nice lemons for this time of year; I'll give you one."

"Why, thank you, Mr. Norton." Mama puts the lemon in the bag with the artichoke.

"My pleasure."

It is dusk when Mama and I walk back home. The streetlights are on. Mama probably has spent more money than she wanted to because of me. And she hasn't even asked me for her change yet. I am so thankful. I decide not to say anything on the way back home. Not talk her ear off.

When we get to our front yard, Mama turns to me and says, "Remember, people will treat you like a dog if you let them. Always treat people the way you want to be treated." Then she kisses me on the forehead.

"That goes for your sister Angela too. I know she isn't perfect, but you don't want her to remember you as a wicked sister, do you?"

23

"No, ma'am."

"'Cause if you do, she'll think you're as prickly as this artichoke that I bought and have no idea what to do with," she says, laughing.

SPIT

Ladies do not spit. It is only two weeks later, and Mama starts in on me and I am not even in the front hall good yet. She says she has told me this before— many times. But I guess I didn't hear her. She says only men and boys spit, and even then it is common and disgusting. She says she has told Curtis to stop spitting, as this will make him seem like one of those hard "block" boys who are delinquents and hang out on the corner downtown. There was Curtis spitting on the playground like he was chewing tobacco and aiming at a spittoon. That's what Mrs. Mumby told Mama. The hag said that I was bouncing around like a jumping bean, my skirt flapping up and down. She told Mama that I will be "ruint" if I don't stop trying to hang out on the basketball court.

Now I can't go out for a week. It is torture. Mrs. Mumby is a witch.

3

FLYING ROCKET

I throw myself onto the double bed that I share with my baby sister and bury my face in the pillow. Mama and Daddy say that after they pay for the new gas furnace, they are going to buy us bunk beds. I'll get to sleep on top. We have already settled that.

I'm glad my sisters aren't here right now. Angela went out to the grocery store with Daddy, picking up everything Mama forgot this time. Diana is at some kind of practice, either cheerleading or choir or with the "Rockets." That's a club she has with some of her high-school girlfriends. They get together and pretend they are grown and talk. Doesn't make sense to me: What color sneakers are they going to wear with their matching pedal pushers? Who's going to make their matching blouses? Which hairstyle would be best with a V neckline—a French twist or a bun on top of the head with fringe curls pulled down in front and back? Mostly they play records and practice the new dances. Mama says I can't go in the living room when it's Diana's turn to have the meeting. But I go anyway and hide behind the couch and steal peanuts and those little pink-and-green mints and drink up the punch.

The last time my sister had the Rockets meeting, I was hiding behind the couch and they were just getting to the good part when an accident happened. It wasn't my fault.

There were five girls including Diana, who was putting a stack of 45 records on the new stereophonic turntable that Daddy saved and saved for and bought just for her. They were sitting around, that's all. Sandy was on the left end of the couch. She is tall and wore tight pants and a sweater set with the cardigan over her shoulders. Sandy always shimmies her shoulders when somebody says or does something she thinks is "outta sight." Lorraine is what Mama calls petite. She looks no bigger than me in her tiny skirt, bobby socks, saddle shoes, and sweater with the high school's team name on it in big raised letters: HORNETS. Patsy reminds me of some of the women in those old movies, sitting straight in her chair with her legs crossed, one hand draped over her leg, the other hand spread across her chest. Every time someone says something that is supposed to be funny, she doesn't laugh; she draws her shoulders back, raises her eyebrows, and says, "Paa-leeez!" Connie is my big sister's best friend. At the meeting that afternoon they both wore tight khaki pants and their cardigan sweaters backward with the buttons up the back and the sleeves pushed up to their elbows and sunglasses. Indoors. Diana also wore a beret and her silky hair in one very long braid over her shoulder.

And they got going. *"Mister Postman, look and see if there's a letter . . . for me?"* They did the mashed potato, the Watusi, the bird. Jumping and hopping and bouncing and dipping. Flinging their arms and snapping their fingers and shaking their hips. Then, *"Come on, baby, do the loco-motion."*

I snuck around the left side of the couch to the coffee table and dipped into the chips and mints, stuffing as much food into my mouth as I could. By the time a couple of records had passed, I had eaten nearly half the chips on repeated trips to the bowl and I needed some of that ginger ale on the other end of the coffee table where the peanuts were. Only I didn't have a glass. *Which glass is Diana's?* I wondered. I looked for a sign of her color lipstick—peach—but they all wore peach lipstick. Peach was one of their club colors.

With hardly a look at me, Sandy sat back down on the couch and took a long drink from her glass and reached for the potato chip bowl. "Humph," she said, wrinkling her nose. "Girl, these chips are disappearing like nobody's business. I'd say there was a mouse in here."

"Yeah, a scrawny, fuzzy-headed one," Connie said, laughing.

"Paa-leeez!" Patsy said.

I scooted back behind the couch. Diana leaned over the back and fussed, "You're not supposed to be in here. Now get on out."

I sat up. "This is my house too, and I can go where I want," I said.

"I'm going to tell Mama."

"So?" I said, crossing my arms across my chest. "I'm gonna tell Mama you been in here dancing nasty."

"I have not," she said.

"Have to. You been doing the dog." I had her there. They had moved from doing the locomotion to seeing who could grind their hips the lowest doing the dog. She rolled her eyes, got off the couch, and went back to the record player, adding another stack of 45s. They danced some more and the more they danced, the thirstier I got. Now the room was starting to get hot and smell like something made up of stale Avon perfume, itchy wool sweaters, hair cream, sweat, and runny makeup. Finally, they fell into a clump on the couch.

"Guess who I saw walking down the hall with his arm around Gina?" Lorraine asked.

Sandy jumped to her feet and put her hands on her hips. "Gina? That streety girl?"

"Now wait a minute, wait a minute, let me finish," Lorraine said, sipping her ginger ale. "It was George Quincy."

"George Quincy!" they all screamed.

"I think he is so fine," Connie said, holding her arms to her chest and squeezing her eyes shut. "Mmm, that wavy hair. I believe he's prettier than Valentine."

Sandy held up a finger to shush everybody. "But what was he doing with her?" she asked.

"Walking her to English class," Lorraine said, sweeping her left arm through the air, "*and* carrying her books."

"No!" They all gasped.

"But, Lorraine, haven't you been eyeing him?" Patsy asked.

"I was," Lorraine said. "Let me finish. Gina went on in and sat down, and he looked up and saw me. Of course, I was pretending that he didn't even exist. So he blocked the doorway and said, 'How are you today, beautiful?' And I said, 'As ever. How are you?' And he said, 'In ecstasy now that I've had the pleasure of seeing your lovely face this morning.' But I didn't fall for it. I looked at him as blankly as I could, so he decided to try harder. He said, 'I couldn't think of anything more pleasurable than if you would allow me to escort you to the game on Friday night.' Well, I was thrilled, but I didn't want to let him know it. So I said, 'I am a Rocket, a sophisticated lady.' Then I glanced across the room at that Miss Gina Thing, primping in her seat, and he said . . ."

At that moment Patsy poured herself another glass of ginger ale and there was hardly any left. She set the bottle down on the right end of the coffee table. I couldn't reach it without coming from around the right side of the couch. The coffee table sat on a small rug. If I pulled on it ever so slowly and slid it across the wood floor, maybe I could reach the bottle. The first time I tugged, it moved a bit.

Then some more. A bit more. Then it stopped, but I still couldn't reach the bottle. I lay on my side and pulled harder. It didn't budge. I sucked in a big breath, braced my feet against the legs of the couch, gave the rug a big strong yank, and that's when it happened. Connie, who had just sat on the end of the table, went flying left, I went flying right, and everything else—potato chips, peanuts, mints, glasses, ice, ginger ale, and Mama's flowered centerpiece with the seashells that Auntie Gert brought all the way back from her cruise to the Virgin Islands— went up in the air, then crashed down on the table. And the floor. And Connie. And Sandy. Before I could recover, Diana had grabbed me by the ear and was crying, *"Mama! Mama!"* Then her friends started grabbing hold of me. I felt like I was in the middle of a stampede, like you see in a cowboy movie.

SOLO

Diana says she never wants to see me again. But that will be hard unless she sleeps outdoors, and I *know* she won't do that. She can't stand bugs. Even though I have told her that they won't hurt you, she doesn't believe me. "Ladybugs can't bite you; they just eat the aphids on the rosebushes," I said, holding up a fat one last summer. But she just screamed, "Get that thing out of *my* room!" Her room? Am I invisible?

I've also told her that daddy longlegs and Japanese beetles won't hurt you either. Heck, even a great big old fat bumblebee won't bother you unless you bother him. But she still hollers for me to squash them for her. I used to. Leaping around the house after moths and spiders and flies. But I don't do that anymore because I am convinced that they are just little animals like a little bitty cat or a little bitty dog and that if you treat them right, they will be your friend.

4

GREEN

Green is a perfectly okay color for grass and vegetables and leaves. It might be fun for an ink pen
color or the shutters on your house or a lizard. But
it is mostly icky. When someone is green, they are
sick. Green vegetables taste raw and horrible.
Green people are either Martians or jealous.

My tongue is green. I have been sitting at the
dining-room table licking S&H Green Stamps and
pasting them into a coupon book. These little
stamps are like money. Every time you buy groceries
at Swan's Market, you get S&H Green Stamps with
your receipt. If you collect enough of them, you can
buy stuff downtown at a special gift store. We need
a new radio. The old one quit—cackled and sputtered for the very last time a month ago. Until then
a good thump could sometimes bring it back to life.

Now Daddy can't listen to the ball games. Diana
and Curtis can't hear the afternoon teen dance

shows. Mama can't hear the news and the gospel hour. And how am I going to practice my dance steps? Daddy says, "If it isn't one thing, it's another," and shoves his hands back into his pockets. I wonder if I am ever going to have my own bed.

"If I had to be a color, I would be pink," I say, wondering how long it will take us to fill up the thirty coupon books that we need to get a new radio. We have seven completed.

Mama overhears me talking to myself. "What's wrong with brown skin?"

"Brown?" I ask, washing my hands in the kitchen sink. Even the soap bubbles are green. "Oh. But I'm beige," I say.

"Brown, beige, black—it doesn't matter what skin you're in," she says.

ANSWERED PRAYER

I am down on my knees in Sunday school, listening to Deaconess Harris pray—". . . Thank you, Lord, for letting me wake up this morning. . . . Thank you, Lord, for giving me the strength to come over here and work with these children, 'cause they need all the help they can get . . ."—when something hits me on the shoulder. I open one eye and see that it is a note.

As quietly as I can, I unfold it: *Meet me after Sun. sch.* I look in the direction that the note must have come from and see Lenore staring at me. "Me?" I mouth, unsure that the message has found its target. She nods her head up and down.

God is good, I think. *God is good.*

OFFERING

I rush and get Angela from her classroom—nearly dragging her up the stairs to the sanctuary where Mama is waiting with Diana. I shove Angela forward.

"Quit!" she yells.

Mama, who is talking to an usher, wraps her arms around Angela and looks at me. I turn to go. "Just where do you think you're going, miss?" she asks.

"To get a drink of water before the service," I say sweetly, and escape. There are things that I just know: No one will deny you a drink of water. Water is good for you and it's nearly free. That makes saying you're thirsty one of the best tactics for getting away.

There's always a lot of commotion going on downstairs at the end of the hall, where an old, leftover pew sits beside the water fountain. That's where most kids—except the Jordans—congregate after Sunday school. People are pushing and shoving, smacking and crying, ranking and laughing. Sometimes the ushers have to come down here and tell the kids, "Hush!"

"Aww!"

"See there!"

But as soon as the usher leaves, you hear:

"You better not."

"I double dare you."

Mama usually gives us "the look" when we pass this section of the downstairs hallway.

A bunch of kids crowd around, waiting as long as possible before they have to go up for morning service. Lenore, of course, is right in the middle. I don't go up to the pew right away. I move slowly down the hall, wrapping and unwrapping my handkerchief around my index finger. My offering—the remainder of my weekly allowance of fifty cents—is tied up in a corner of it.

Ce-Ce sits on one side of Lenore, Nadine on the other. There's Cubie and Patricia and too many others to name. They are all knotted up like a ball of rerolled yarn.

Lenore looks up and motions for me to come. She shoves Nadine over and pats the spot beside her on the pew. Though I can feel Nadine burning a hole in my neck with a stare as hot as Superman's

X-ray eyes, here I am sitting side by side with Lenore. We're smooshed together like we're best friends. Never mind that I thought it would be just her and me. Never mind that we aren't even talking. Not that I have anything to say. Everyone else jaws on and on about one thing or another:

"Deaconess Harris does *too* wear a wig."

"How you know?"

"'Cause I seen them gray beady plaits up under the edge."

"Aww!"

Lenore holds up her hand and says sweetly, "What about the movies, you all? Are we going?"

Then they start talking about new ones and old ones. I keep wrapping and unwrapping my finger, just happy to be here. A prayer answered.

"I like James Bond in *Dr. No.*"

"That was cool, but wasn't it scary in *The Time Machine* when he couldn't get back?"

"Not really. Now, *The Mummy's Hand* was scary when that hand got the man around the throat."

"Humph. That's nothing. *Psycho* was scarier than anything I've ever seen."

"Oh, you ain't see no *Psycho*! They don't let no kids see that."

Lenore holds up a hand again to shush folks. "I said: Are we going? If so, pony up." She puts her hat in her lap.

Kids start tossing coins in the hat. "Hmm, doesn't look like enough for bus fare, let alone movie tickets," Lenore says.

Cubie and the rest of them start grumbling, pulling pocket liners inside out and letting them hang like dog's ears.

"Shoot!" Ce-Ce says, looking into the hat. "And it's my turn to go too."

I look around and find myself staring at Nadine, her lips poked out. I don't know what has gotten into me, but I stick out my tongue.

I turn back around and find Lenore looking at me. At first I don't get it. She has to come right out and ask: "How much you got?"

I have a nickel and a dime. I have already put one dime in the Sunday-school collection. "Fifteen cents," I say. I unwrap the handkerchief and ball it up in my hand, hiding it in plain sight. Everyone stares at my hand. Finally, I unknot the corner and drop in the coins, wondering what I will do when the offering plate is passed upstairs.

Lenore smiles and hugs me. It makes me feel

a little better. "That'll help," she says, shoving the hat at me. "You count it up. I hear you're good in math."

"Okay. Ten . . . forty . . . eighty-five . . . one dollar and thirty . . . one dollar and seventy-three cents," I announce.

"Okay," Lenore says, "fifteen cents for bus fare and twenty-five cents for the movies." She starts trying to put the coins into little piles. I can see that this won't work. I add the bus and movie costs in my head, then divide and say: "It's enough for four people to go."

Heads snap.

"Well, with thirteen cents left over," I add.

Lenore looks up. "That means, Nadine, you go next time. Okay?"

"Dag!" Nadine says, and folds her arms and rolls her eyes.

"Aww, girl," Cubie says, doing an air swipe across Nadine's head, "you're always going on somebody else's dime. You ought to ask your granddaddy to get up off of some of that Cadillac money."

Then Lenore says to me, "Pearl, you have to pay your dues first." And I know what she means. But I am relieved. Going to the movies on a Sunday—the

Lord's Day? I would never hear the end of it. Mama would preach for weeks.

Suddenly, the organ prelude begins, and everyone stampedes down the hall and up the stairs. Curtis and Diana sit on either side of Mama, who has Angela on her lap. Daddy sits with the choir. Mama ignores me as I slip in beside Curtis. This is worse than the evil eye. I touch my shoulders where Lenore hugged me, but I have a knot in my stomach. As soon as the offering plate is passed, Mama will know. A thought comes to me: *I will not buy candy next week.* Next Sunday, I will put my entire allowance in the plate.

I hope I don't have to buy pencils at school.

5

DOUBLE-CROSSED

The phone rings. I know who it is. Ever since I hung out with her two Sundays ago on the church hall bench, Lenore has started calling me after school. Mama doesn't like it. Every time Lenore calls, Mama has something for me to do. "Is the living room dusted and the stuff picked up in there?" she'll ask.

"Yes," I answer.

"Have you finished getting the laundry off the clothesline? Is everything folded and put away? What about your ironing, young lady? I'm not raising any lazy children around here."

"Yes. Yes. Yes."

When the phone rings this time, Mama is busy with dinner. She has several pots going at once.

"I got it, Ma!" I run into the hall to pick up the phone.

"What'chu doing?" Lenore asks, her singsong voice whispering over the line.

"Nothing," I say.

"You want to come down and play?"

"Well, I want to, but I've got to finish—" I stop short. I don't really want to tell Lenore that I'm pasting green stamps. "I've got to finish dusting," I say.

"Dusting?" Lenore says.

Oh, shoot. That sounded so uncool. I quickly change the subject. "Can you come up here?" I ask.

"I don't think so," Lenore whispers. "I haven't even started my homework, and my mother would kill me if she knew I was on the phone. I snuck out of church on Sunday and went to the movies early. I'm not supposed to use the phone for a week. Uh-oh. Here she comes. I'll call you back."

"Okay," I say, and hang up quickly. A week ago, when it was my turn to go to the movies from the "collection," I made the mistake of asking Mama. Of course she said, "No."

"But when can I go?" I whined.

"When you save up your money, you can go with your brother and sister on Saturdays, like always," I remember her saying as plain as day, even though I had cried and jumped up and down and even tried to work her with "You never let me do anything!"

I set the phone back on the hall table, go back to

the kitchen, and plop down on the chair at the table, where I am drowning in a sea of green. "Why can't Diana do some of this?" I moan.

"She isn't even here," Mama says, switching from the steaming pot of kale to her secret breading for liver. "While you're complaining, you could have finished another page," she says, emphasizing every word with a nod of a long-handled spoon. "I've already done three books today myself. You should be able to do at least one."

I groan and pretend to be sick to my stomach. She ignores me.

"Who were you talking to?"

"When?"

"Just now, silly."

"Oh, only Lenore," I say. "She wanted me to come play." I hope Mama will take the big hint and release me from my prisoner's chair. But she doesn't bite. So I act like I don't want to go to Lenore's. "But I told her that I had to finish something first."

Mama raises her brows and rolls her eyes.

After I finish one book of stamps, I pull out my book bag. Thank goodness I have a lot of home-work to do. Sitting right there at the kitchen table,

I finish my math in a jiffy. Math never gives me any problems. It's so logical. Things just grow, shrink, or get divided up into groups. While the rest of the kids in the class are sweating it out— carrying over numbers, lining up columns, and bringing numbers down—I already have the answer. The rest of my homework is easy too. I conjugate my verbs and read two chapters in my American history book.

"Mom, I finished my homework," I announce. She is up to her wrists in flour biscuits. But before I can ask to go play, she comes up with one of her instant requests.

"Where's your sister?" she asks without looking up.

"I don't know," I say smartly. But as soon as I say that, I know I shouldn't have.

My mother looks at me, ready to spring if I breathe wrong. "Well, you better make it your business to find out."

"Yes, ma'am."

I run down the hall to the bottom of the front stairs. "Angela! Angela!" I call up. I hear little steps on the landing. My sister appears in a pink princess dress, Mama's high heels and pearls, a feather boa around her neck, and her Barbie doll cradled in her arm. She has undone her braids and combed her hair into a tangled mess.

"What're you doing!" I say in a loud whisper. "Mama would be mad if she knew you were fooling with her stuff!"

"I'm not doing anything," she says, putting one hand on her hip. Then she flings her hair over her shoulder and begins brushing it with Mama's ivory-handled brush from her fancy dresser set. We aren't allowed to go near the pretty things on Mama's dresser—the things that Uncle Albert brought back for her from Korea.

Instead of tattling, I push her into our bedroom. "Sit down and let me try to straighten out the mess on your head."

"You're not the boss of me," she says.

"No, but Mama's going to wear your little bottom out if she sees you looking like a wild woman and fooling with her stuff," I say, reaching for the biggest comb I can find on our dresser.

"She doesn't care," Angela says, poking her lips out at me.

"Wanna bet? You try waltzing yourself downstairs and you'll find out. Now sit here on the floor."

Angela thinks about that and sits down. I perch on the edge of the bed with her head and shoulders between my knees and try to fish through the tangles. Mama is very particular. She combs and braids our hair every day. She doesn't like it if she has to spend extra time untangling it. It makes her late for picking up her bookkeeping work.

Angela's hair looks like a bird's nest. "Owww! Owww!" She whimpers and cries and pulls away several times. "Owww! Owww! You're hurting me," she cries again.

We hear footsteps pause at the bottom of the stairs. "What's going on up there?" Mama calls. Angela jumps onto the bed behind me.

"Nothing," I yell. "We're just playing." Angela and I both hold our breath to see if we can hear her come up the stairs. She doesn't. "Come on," I say, "I'm not near finished."

"Okay, okay," she says, sliding quickly back onto the floor.

I get the top part loose enough to braid, though not anywhere as smooth as Mama does it. My fingers fly—over, under, over, under. I start combing the back. "Hold still!" I say. When I begin to part it into two long braids, she jumps and yells.

"Ahhh!" She knocks over the dresser chair with her feet and starts crying buckets of tears.

"What are you all doing up there?" Mama yells from downstairs. "It sounds like you're coming through the ceiling!"

"We were playing and we accidentally tipped over the chair, that's all," I say, motioning for Angela to stop crying. But she doesn't. She cries louder.

"I don't want to have to come up there!" Mama calls. She starts up the stairs and Angela finally freezes. Then Mama stops. "Oh, Lord, the liver!" I hear her run back to the kitchen.

Angela sits back down on the floor, still crying. "It doesn't hurt this bad when Mama does it," she whines.

"Well, I'm not Mama," I say, my fingers working. She hits me every time I come to a kink, so I just leave the snarls, braid it up, and snap on the final barrette. "Get those shoes and that necklace," I say, picking up Mama's ivory brush.

"But I'm not finished playing with them," Angela says.

"You are now," I say. I pull her by the hand and

creep down the hall. We slip into Mama's room. The wardrobe is open and Mama's heels are scattered all over. Her top dresser drawer is hanging open, her jewelry piled in a heap on top. Daddy's newly pressed shirts are knocked off their hangers and lying on the floor. It takes Mama all morning long to starch and iron Daddy's white shirts. She would have a fit if she saw all this. I should leave it and let Angela get into trouble. Then I imagine the punishment. We—yes, we, because somehow Angela is always *my* responsibility—we wouldn't get to watch TV or go to the movies or use the telephone for I don't know how long. So I help Angela put the shoes back, rehang the shirts, and try to straighten out the jewelry. But I can't figure out which boxes go with which necklaces, earrings, and bracelets. I arrange it all as best I can, close the dresser drawer, and turn to leave. Mama's bedspread, the white chenille one with the pink, red, and blue roses, is all twisted up in the center.

"Have you been jumping on the bed again too?" I ask.

Angela looks at me shamefaced.

I smooth the bedspread.

We start down the stairs and meet Mama on her way up.

"Set the table," my mother says to me, and turns around, heading back to the kitchen.

"Yes, ma'am," I say. I pull a tablecloth out of the sideboard drawer, take it into the dining room, and spread it out in the air, letting it land directly on top of the table. As I gather up six plates from the kitchen, it dawns on me that Miss Angela is sitting there on her duff and that I have just saved her from getting her bottom smacked. "How come she isn't helping?" I ask my mother.

"She is," Mama says. "Angela, get the knives and forks."

But my baby sister doesn't budge. She is fiddling with the paper dolls that she keeps in her doll carriage beside the cupboard.

"Angela," I call. She doesn't move. When I come back to the cupboard for napkins, she is still dressing and undressing dolls. "Angela!" I reach for her arm, but she pulls away.

"You'd better leave me alone," she says, "or I'm telling."

That gets Mama's attention.

"Telling what?" Mama asks.

"That Pearl was fooling with your things," she says.

"Me?" I ask, amazed.

"What things?" Mama asks, looking at me as if *I* am the guilty one.

"Your shoes and your brush and your powder puff, your lipstick, and your . . . your bobby pins. And your hair net," Angela says, starting to make it up as she goes along.

"I did not," I say. "*You* were up there fooling with her stuff and *I* put it all back."

"Angela," Mama says, picking her up, "you better not be telling a tale."

"I'm not," Angela says.

"Not even a little bit?" Mama asks, hugging her.

"Well, I was wearing your pink shoes is all. And I tried on your gloves."

"I see," Mama says. "Well, when I tell you not to mess up my things, I mean that. Do you understand?"

"Uh-huh," Angela says.

"Now put your dolls away and help Pearl finish setting the table."

"Okay," Angela says, kissing Mama and sliding down to the floor. She skips over to the drawer and grabs a handful of silverware.

When I was six, Mama never would have let me get away with fibbing like that without a spanking.

I will have to lie beside Angela tonight. And I'll have a hard time falling asleep, thinking about how she double-crossed me—and about how *I* would have been the baby if she hadn't come along.

6

ESCAPE

All that evening and the next day it worries me that Lenore hasn't called back. Does that mean she won't be my friend anymore? I just keep thinking about it while I try to show Angela how to bowl in the hallway. I roll the ball into the plastic bowling pins, knocking most of them down.

"Angela, it's still my turn," I say, taking the ball from her.

"But you had a turn."

"I know, but I get a second turn."

"You're just making that up," she says.

"No, I'm not. Those are the rules."

"How do you know?"

Mama, who is doing her bookkeeping, peers around the corner to where we sit. "Yes, Pearl, how do you know? There isn't a bowling alley in this town that allows any colored people. We have to go clear to Washington, D.C., to go bowling."

I can't stand it when Mama says "colored." It sounds so old-timey. Mrs. Scott in school says we are "Negroes." "It's 'Negroes,' Mama. 'Negroes.' Besides, I've seen bowling on TV. You get two chances to knock down the pins."

"Oh," Mama says. "Miss Smarty-pants." Then she goes back to her bookkeeping.

"Yeah," Angela says, "Miss Smarty-pants."

I hiss at Angela. I always have to stop and explain everything to her because she is younger. I know she can't help that, so I give her the ball. The fun has gone out of the game. I get up and walk to the end of the hall and look out the front door. The top half has a window with flowers etched in the glass around the sides. I gaze out onto the front porch, then out into the front yard, then out into the street at cars and buses passing on a Friday evening. In another hour or so the traffic will pick up with people coming home from work in Washington. Daddy will be on one of those buses. He gets off just up at the corner. I wish he were here now. Maybe I could talk to him. I used to talk to Grandma, who was my mother's mother. She lived out on the edge of town. When Mama was going back to school, I used to spend afternoons with her and her two dogs, Comet and Cupid. I remember telling her there was a monster under my bed. At night I had to leap from the floor onto the bed so he wouldn't grab my feet. It is the same bed that I share with Angela. I turn around, and Angela has left and taken her dolls that go where she goes. But the pins and ball are scattered everywhere. I walk back down the hall, but instead of picking up the toys, I dial Lenore's number. *If her mother answers, I'll just hang up*, I think. The phone rings only a half time before someone answers it:

"If you've got the dime, I've got the time!"

I laugh, then cup my hand over my mouth and whisper, "It's me."

"What'chu doing?" Lenore asks.

"Nothing," I whisper.

"Can you come over?"

"I don't know." I put my hand over the mouth of the receiver and peek around the corner. My mother is taking a break from her bookkeeping and reading the afternoon paper. "Let me see," I say, putting the phone down and going into the kitchen.

"Can I go to Lenore's?"

Mama keeps reading. "Aren't you playing with your sister?" she asks.

"Not really. She just wants to play dolls and stuff."

"So play dolls," Mama says.

"Well, I don't like to play dolls."

Mama looks up. "I'm not going to be chasing you all over this neighborhood."

"I'm not going to be all over the neighborhood. I'm just going to be at Lenore's. I won't be long."

She twists around in her seat and blows out a big breath, like I am irritating her and she would be glad to get me out of her hair for a while. She pushes the newspaper aside and grabs the mound of bookkeeping folders. "All right. But be back in time to set the table."

I rush out the back door. "That's only an hour from now," she calls after me.

DINK

As I am walking by Dink's house, I get a little bit of a sinking feeling. I hope he isn't hiding behind the hedges waiting for me to pass on my way to Lenore's to pop me in the head with a rock.

He is. He comes down his driveway on roller skates as I try to scoot down the street and turn the corner.

"Hey, bird legs!" he calls. I run faster, but he follows me, pelting me with gravel as I try to cover

55

my head. There ought to be a law. For someone so small, he can really move.

"Get away from me, you pest!" I scream behind me. Now I am getting all sweaty. My bra is beginning to make me itch.

"You knock-kneed bony-maroney," he calls.

"I am *not* knock-kneed," I manage to say. He is just inches behind me. When he finally catches up, I give him the stiff arm, and down he goes, crying and carrying on.

He lets out a blast of cuss words, which I am not going to repeat. Then he finishes it off with, "I'm gonna get you, Olive Oyl!"

7

THE SECRET

Lenore and I sit on her front porch, riding back and forth on her metal glider rocker. We sit up high on the big, fat pillows. The glider squeaks as we ride forward, then bangs into the wall as we go backward. *Squeak. Bang!* Lenore shoves the glider as hard as she can, her hands in the air as if she's on a roller coaster. I am along for the ride. She whips her hair around. Her mother lets her get it cut, straightened, and curled at the beauty shop. She is allowed to wear it down every day. It looks so grown up. I pull on my thick ropey braid, slip the ribbon off the end, and put it into my pocket. Ribbons seem kind of babyish right about now.

"Lenore!" her mother screams down onto the roof of the porch from the bathroom window upstairs. "What are you doing down there?" We put our feet on the porch floor and grind the big glider to a halt.

"Nothing!" Lenore screams back.

"Did you finish your homework?"

"Yes, ma'am," Lenore answers. But she didn't. I finished it.

"Can you show me how to do this math problem?" Lenore asked.

"Sure," I said, eager to display my arith-magician skills.

Before I laid down the pencil, she asked, "What about this one?"

"Okay." The next thing I knew, I had done all one hundred of the math problems. All fifty words in the puzzle. All of the questions in the geography quiz.

We hear Mrs. Robinson close the window.

"Humph," Lenore says. "Adults invented homework to keep you from having any fun your whole life." She stands up and grabs her ring binder notebook off the white metal table and throws it up in the air. Then she tosses up her math book and her pencils and her Bambi pencil sharpener and her tub of erasers. And it all comes crashing down on the cement floor of the porch—swishes, scatters, and rolls. The cover tears off of her book.

I cringe, but she looks at me and grins. "I can't

wait till I'm grown and I can do stuff and be with people and stay up late and have fun. All I ever do is feed the cats and the hamsters, practice the piano, go to ballet class, sing in the stupid old choir, recite some dumb poem in a play, and go to charm school." She flops down on the seat cushion, her school skirt settling over her knees. She throws her head back and laughs. I laugh too. Lenore is some daredevil. I cross my legs, press my jeans smooth over my legs, and sit up straight.

"You're so lucky. You don't have to do any of that," she tells me.

But I don't feel lucky. I want pets, piano lessons, ballet slippers, to be chosen for the choir. I want my own electric train set, seeing as how I am not even allowed to touch my brother's. I want my own bike and not my brother's hand-me-down. I have asked for all of these things, but nobody pays any attention to me. I never get anything that I want. "I'll feed the cats and hamsters for you," I say.

"Those nasty old things," she says.

"I don't think they're nasty," I say. But I could have been talking to a wall. She doesn't even answer me. After a while I ask, "Well, what do you want to do?"

"What do you want to do?" she answers.

"You want to play jacks?" I offer, knowing good and well that Lenore would think basketball was only for boys.

She scrunches up her face in disgust.

"Well, you want to jump rope?"

She shakes her head. Then she turns to me with a devilish grin on her face. "I know," she says, "let's play hand-jive. I learned a new one in school today."

We turn to face each other, holding our palms out, then clap and start slapping each other's palms as she sings with a one-two beat:

"Marguerite got stinky feet,
she got dirty drawers
and rotten teeth.
When the girls went out to play,
they said, Marguerite, girl,
stay away!"

I howl as we clap out the last line. "You learned that at school?" I ask.

"Yeah, a girl taught me on the playground. She told me some others, too, but I don't remember them too good. They go something like:

"You bring the nickel,
I'll bring the dime.
We'll put it all together
and have a good time.
One for the candy,
one for the show.
Come on, girl,
go, girl, go!

"How did that other one go?" Lenore says, still holding her hands up. "Oh, yeah.

"Shake it to the east,
shake it to the west.
Shake it to the one
that you love best!"

Just then Lenore's mother opens the front door. "Lenore! What are you doing?"

I jump off the glider and stand up. Lenore stays seated, still facing me with her back to her mother, and rolls her eyes. "Nothing," she says. I assume her mother will make her turn around, but she doesn't.

"Well, it sounds like you need your mouth

washed out with soap. Do not let me hear you carrying on like that again."

"Yes, ma'am," Lenore says, grinning, her back still turned.

It is a delayed reaction when Mrs. Robinson notices the pencils, papers, erasers, and books littering the floor. At first I think she's going to have a cow. Before she can say anything, Lenore swivels around and says, "I tripped over the table. I really banged up my shin. Clumsy me."

"Are you all right?" Mrs. Robinson says, bending over and rubbing Lenore's leg.

"I think I'll be okay. I was just waiting for the pain to quit before I picked up all my stuff."

"Oh, sweetie," Mrs. Robinson says. "Let me know if it swells up." She looks at me and leaves.

"Come on," Lenore whispers. "Let's go up to my room. She can't hear so good up there when I close the door."

Lenore has a white four-poster bed with a matching white-and-pink canopy and curtains. Pink ballet slippers are tied to one post, and her ballet tights and tutu hang on the front of her closet. She has her very own dresser with lots of things on it, like a jewelry box with a ballerina that spins around to a pretty song when you open it. She even has one of those porcelain dolls from China in a glass case.

A hamster is running on a wheel in his cage. I want to go pick him up. But Lenore lies facedown on the bed, so I do the same. Then she reaches in the drawer of her nightstand and takes out a book. She turns over and holds it up and lets something drop to her chest. "Look what I've got," she says, holding up a small piece of paper.

"What?" I ask.

"It's a secret. A picture of a boy."

"Where'd you get that?"

"In school, goofy," she says.

"Oh, yeah," I say.

"Don't you have a boyfriend?" she asks.

"No," I say.

"Well, don't you have pictures of boys?"

"No."

"Well, what do you do in school all day?"

"Study, I guess."

"Well, I don't. I pass notes to Robby. That's his name."

"I could never get away with that in Mrs. Scott's class," I say. "She can even see around corners." I sneak a look at the picture that Lenore has above her chest. It is a boy all right. But he doesn't look any different from any other boys I have ever seen. He has closely clipped hair, big ears, and a toothy grin. "What do you write in the notes?" I ask.

"I can't tell you that," she says.

I am disappointed because I can't imagine what a note would say. "Oh, please," I beg.

"Well, you promise you won't tell?"

"Cross my heart and hope to die," I say, crossing my chest with my right hand.

"Well, I just tell him I like him and stuff," she says, giggling.

I nod my head, but I really don't get it.

"You know," she says.

I nod again.

"Like today he wrote: 'Can you sit beside me at lunch? I want to ask you something.' So I wrote back and said: 'Yes, if I can keep the teacher from seeing me switch places in line.'"

I nod some more.

"So I switched places with Arlene and we sat together," she says, gushing.

"So, what did he ask you?"

"What?" Lenore asks, as if she has forgotten what we are talking about.

"What did he ask you?" I repeat.

She looks at me as though I should already know, but I don't. "He wanted to know if he could have my dessert."

I nod. "Did you let him?"

"Of course."

"Well, what did you eat?"

"What do you mean?"

"I mean, what dessert did you eat?"

"None, silly."

"Why?" I ask.

"You don't know anything," she says, playfully slapping my hand. "When you like a boy, you like him."

"Oh," I say, nodding. But I don't really understand. I turn over and stare up at the canopy. We don't talk any more. She reaches for a basket filled with magazines, *Highlights* and *Jack and Jill,* and we look through those together. Then her mother comes into the room. "Pearl, your mother called. She said you need to come home right now."

"Thanks, Mrs. Robinson," I say, sliding off the bed. Lenore follows me to the front door. "See you," I say.

"Okay," she answers, and waves. I walk back

home, past Miss Lela's, past Dink's house, and into my yard. Nobody has ever told me a secret before. Lenore is some friend.

YELLOW

She is minding a bunch of little kids, the girl in the yellow dress. I stare at her across the playground. I have just finished Lenore's homework, and Lenore and I need someone else to turn so we can jump rope. Ce-Ce had to stay after school, and Nadine's grandmother is making her wash windows.

"What about her?" I say, pointing across the basketball court.

"Oh, that old stanky girl," Lenore says, wrinkling up her nose.

"How do you know that she smells?"

"Look at her. Last year's Easter dress up to her thighs." Lenore laughs.

The girl does look funny in a yellow print chiffon dress on the playground. She has on sneakers without socks. Her arms are bare, though it is still cool for early April. She is wiping the snotty noses of the little kids around her legs when she looks up and catches me staring. I quickly look away. I look around the playground and, in an instant, see that there are no other girls near our age who would want to join us. We can see that clearly.

"Just this once," I say, winding and unwinding the rope around my hand.

"Well, you go and get her, then," Lenore says. "I'm not going."

"Okay." I toss my jacket on the ground and walk up to the yellow chiffon girl. There is something familiar about her.

"Hi," I say.

She steps back. "Hi," she says. The little kids cling to her arms and legs. Two girls and a little boy. They all have the same face except hers is larger. Round and dark with eyes as big as quarters. Her skin is smooth like black marble and stands out against the pale yellow dress. I want to ask why she is wearing that dress—on a school day, on the playground—but instead I ask if she wants to jump rope.

"Yeah," she says. The little kids follow us back to Lenore, then I remember I don't know her name and ask.

"Artemesia," she answers. I tell her mine and Lenore's. Artemesia just nods her head.

She's a good turner. We both turn while Lenore jumps and shoots off her mouth. The little kids just sit in the grass and giggle with their hands over their mouths.

> *"Down in the meadow*
> *where the green grass grows,*
> *there sat Annie,*
> *sweet as a rose.*
> *She sang, she sang,*
> *she sang so sweet,*
> *along came Johnny*
> *and kissed her on the cheek.*
> *How many kisses did she get?*
> *One, two, three, four . . ."*

Lenore shakes her butt and carries on until she gets tired. Then it is my turn.

> *"Last night*
> *and the night before*
> *twenty-four robins came knocking at my door.*
> *I went down*
> *to let them in,*
> *they hit me on the head*

with a rolling pin.
How many hits
did I get?
One, two, three, four, five . . ."

I finally jump out at eighty-nine. Nadine shows up. I don't know why, but Lenore asks Nadine if she wants to jump next. "But it's Artemesia's turn," I say.

"Oh," Lenore says, and snickers with Nadine like I am not there. I don't like it when Lenore acts like that. She only does that when other people are around. Artemesia, who had been laughing, now stands quietly, shifting from one foot to the other with her head bowed. It seems like the longest time. So awkward. Then Artemesia begins turning the rope, and Lenore starts up too. Nadine jumps in.

"Cinderella
dressed in yellow
went outside
to kiss a fellow.
By mistake
she kissed a snake.
How many doctors did it take?
Two, four, six, eight . . ."

Nadine shows her butt for a long time until she stops and says, "I don't want to jump any more."

"Me neither," Lenore says, dropping the rope. They both start walking off. "You coming?" Lenore asks.

How can I leave? How can I not leave? I look at her, then at Artemesia. I bend my wrist back slowly to wave. "Bye," I say.

"Bye," she answers.

8

DIME STORE

I can't believe it. Mrs. Robinson is picking me up in her station wagon, and I'm going with Lenore to the roller rink. I've wanted to go there since it's been integrated, but Mama was always saying no. Then, out of the blue, Mrs. Robinson called yesterday and invited me. Mama sputtered all over herself on the phone as I jumped up and down like I was on a trampoline, then got down on my knees and "walked" around Mama with my hands folded in prayer as she talked to Mrs. Robinson.

"That's so sweet of you to think of Pearl," Mama said into the receiver. "I'll have her ready tomorrow at one o'clock."

Exactly on time, Mrs. Robinson pulls up and blows the horn, and I jerk open the front door, my metal skates flung over my shoulder. Mama is right behind me. "Now, you stay with Mrs. Robinson," she says. "Don't let her out of your sight.

And if anybody bothers you, you tell her."

I am running toward the car in the driveway, Mrs. Robinson at the wheel and Lenore and Nadine and Ce-Ce in back.

Mama is matching my pace, straightening my collar and smoothing my hair. "Here's forty cents for admission and ten cents left over for a soda pop or something." When we reach the car, I jump in back and Mama holds on to the door. "Hello, Jewell," Mama says. "Thanks for letting Pearl come along."

"You're welcome," Mrs. Robinson says. "But she won't need those," she says, pointing to my skates. "They have rink skates there. She can rent some."

"Oh," Mama says. I hand Mama the skates through the window, and Mrs. Robinson starts backing out.

"Jewell, call me if there's any trouble," Mama yells.

"There won't be any trouble," Mrs. Robinson answers.

First off, I cannot believe how big the rink is when we pull up in front. Kids are running up the steps and rushing through the huge doors. Mrs. Robinson stops the car and we pile out. *Maybe she is going to park the car,* I think. Then I hear her call after us. "I'll pick you up at four thirty, at the end of the session," she says, and drives off. When I turn back around, Lenore and Nadine and Ce-Ce have disappeared.

Second, I cannot believe how many people are here. I get swept up in the crowd and shoved around. When I finally make it inside, Lenore is already in the ticket booth line.

"Where's your mom going?" I ask.

"To a club meeting."

"Oh." Children and adults are chattering. The noise echoes off the tall ceilings, metal doors, and marble floors. When we get to the ticket window, the admission and skate rental take all I have—fifty cents. Lenore and Ce-Ce are the only ones with a little change left over.

I try to stay behind them, keeping my eye on Lenore's chesterfield jacket, Ce-Ce's red parka, and Nadine's purple hat and scarf. We are bobbing through a river of kids to pick up our skates. When I finally get mine and drop off my shoes, I stand in the middle of the aisle in my socks. I have no idea where everyone else is. I can't see over the top of this moving stream of people's heads, so I look up. The ceiling is a large dome. It's divided into sections with scenes painted on each one: dancers, acrobats, elephant tamers, jugglers, and clowns. Below that is a bank of windows all the way around. Light floods the rink. Below the windows in one corner is a set of organ pipes. Some are bigger around than a fat man's leg. They are tall and pointy. In another corner, up high, is the organ itself. A man is playing it, and the sounds mix with the noise bouncing around. Then the way in front of me clears and I see the rink floor. It is shiny wood. Looks as big as a football field. People are skating round and round—moving to the perky music.

I am taking all this in when I nearly get knocked flat. A tall, pasty-looking teenage boy runs into me. I stagger and drop my skates.

"Hey, what're you doing? You're blocking the way!" he says as he skates past. Just as I am picking up the skates, someone else grabs my arm, and I find myself spun around. It's Lenore and Nadine and Ce-Ce. They've dumped their coats and put on their skates.

"Girl, we been looking for you. Where you been?" Lenore asks.

"Right here," I say, rubbing my shoulder. It's a little sore. "This place is huge."

"Yeah, isn't it great!" she says.

"Come on. Take off your coat and get your skates on." They rush me in my socks to some chairs on the other side of the rink where they have stashed their coats and pester me to lace my boots in a hurry.

I am the last one through the guardrail opening to the rink floor, and I have to skate fast to keep up with them. I am out of control immediately, but I have no idea how to stop. My feet go right from under me and I land on my butt. Then Ce-Ce falls. And Lenore. And Nadine. We are all on the floor, laughing.

"Wow!" I say to them. "These skates are faster than my metal ones."

"And the floor's so smooth," says Ce-Ce. "It's like you're gliding."

A man in a black-and-white striped shirt skates up to us with a whistle in his mouth. He helps us up and ushers us to the side. "Stay close to the guardrail until you get used to it," he says, and skates off. With our right hands on the rail, we skate along, one behind the other, giggling every time we stumble, looking like Saturday-night drunks.

People are passing us, just bopping and swinging to the music as we slip and bump along. Just as I am getting the hang of it the music stops and people begin to leave the floor.

Another man in a striped shirt comes up and stops us. He doesn't talk, just points to an electric sign. ALL CLEAR, it says. We scramble off the rink at the next exit. I have no idea where our stuff is.

"Isn't this hip?" Lenore says, grabbing us all by the shoulders. We wobble.

"Yeah," says Ce-Ce.

"We should have been coming here a long time ago," Nadine says.

Suddenly, we are stampeded as the music starts up again and people rush back onto the floor. We follow the crowd, going back to the rail single file. Another striped-shirt man comes up to us and points to the sign. This one says, PAIRS. So we pair up. Me and Nadine. Ce-Ce and Lenore. It's hard at first to hold hands and keep our balance. But after a few laps we get the hang of it. I think we are doing fine until I notice some other couples: Men and women skate together as if they are doing ballroom dancing. Men lead women around the rink, turning them and lifting them; then they glide away cheek to cheek. There are even some kids who can do this.

In the center a man catches a woman who leaps through the air, and they spin off.

"Did you see that?" I ask Nadine.

"Sure did," she says, looking at me in amazement. "We got to do better than this," she says, laughing.

Soon I get the hang of skating to the music, and Nadine picks it up too. We're not so much holding on to each other for dear life anymore. We catch up to Lenore and Ce-Ce, who are still struggling, and skate past them, smiling.

"Hey!" Lenore says. "Well, excuse me!"

As we are laughing the rink fills again with tons of people. ALL SKATE, the sign says.

I don't even notice time passing as we skate round and round—trios, pairs, and all skate. We are even good enough now to skate through the gates. The men in the striped shirts are ushers. During intermission they organize races and put on short dance performances with some of the women.

Somehow we find our seats to take a break. It dawns on me, as I look around the crowd, that only a few of the skaters are Negroes. Most of the crowd is white, though no one has picked a fight with us yet.

"I'm thirsty," Nadine says.

"Me too," Lenore, Ce-Ce, and I say together, and this makes us laugh too.

"Come on, let's get something to eat," Lenore says, popping up out of her chair.

"I'm busted," Nadine says.

"Me too," I say. "I don't have a nickel to my name."

"Can you lend me some money, Lenore?" Nadine asks. "I'll pay you back."

Lenore struggles to count her change. Forty cents. "I only have enough for a Coke and a slice of pizza."

"Dag," Nadine says.

I just fold my arms and imagine the pizza that I am not going to get. Or the icy cold bottle of Coca-Cola that won't be dripping with ice crystals in my hand.

Ce-Ce stands up. "I think I have enough for a Coca-Cola."

Nadine and I follow Lenore and Ce-Ce up to the refreshment counter. They have everything there. Hot dogs, half-smoked sausages, pizza, french fries, chili con carne, cheeseburgers, cotton candy, popcorn, candy bars. It smells so good. I look at the price board and quickly figure out that a drink and a slice of pizza will cost thirty-five cents.

"I've got to go to the bathroom," Nadine says, and skates off. Ce-Ce follows her. Lenore and I finally go where they go. I am glad that Lenore doesn't buy food and eat in front of us.

Girls and women are in the bathroom, smoking. We cough and cough. They all rush out when we come in. Nadine skates over to the first stall and yanks the door. It doesn't open.

"Dag, y'all. A pay toilet," she says. "A dime! And I really gotta go too."

We crowd around the lock on the bathroom stall. We check the other two. The middle one has an OUT OF ORDER sign on the stall door.

Ce-Ce holds up her dime and says, "I guess I'm going to drink water." She puts it in the coin slot, opens the stall door, and goes in.

"I have an idea," I say. "We'll all use the same toilet. Just don't let the door close when you come out, Ce-Ce."

"Okay," she says.

"Good thinking, girl," Lenore says. I am feeling fairly clever about this discovery, while Nadine still frets over how we're going to get pizza and drinks.

"It smells so good," she says. "Do you think they'll

just let us have some if we offer to pay them back later?" she asks. No one answers her.

"I know," I say. "We can look for money in the coin return of the pay phone. It's just outside the door."

"Yeah!" Nadine says, clapping her hands.

I scoot out the door and stop myself by grabbing hold of the phone booth. I slip inside the booth and put my fingers in the coin return. It's empty as a bird's nest in the fall.

When I return empty-handed, Nadine says, "Dag!"

Ce-Ce finally finishes getting redressed, and Nadine rolls in before the stall door closes.

Just then a woman comes into the bathroom. She puts a dime in the last stall and goes in. We wait for her to leave before we take turns again. Someone else comes in while I am in the stall. I wait for her to leave before turning the stall over to Lenore. We all finally plop down on the lounge chairs with Lenore saying, "Think, think, think."

"I can't," Ce-Ce says, fanning herself. "The cigarette smoke in here is about to kill me."

"Me too," I say. We stand up to skate out, and Lenore says, "I got it! We'll take the money."

"What?"

"You'll see." She pulls a dime from her pocket,

reopens the first stall, and holds the door open. *Hmm, one less dime*, I think. Two girls come in. The rest of us sit back down in the lounge chairs. Lenore motions for the girls to come to the first stall. "Here," she says. "Those are out of order. I'll take your dimes."

"Says who?" the first girl asks.

"Oh, Mr. Smith," Lenore says. "He asked me to collect the money and give it to him."

"Okay." Both girls hand Lenore a dime and take turns using the toilet. I am amazed that they buy the story so easily. When they leave, we crack up, holding our sides and hooting and hollering.

"Lenore, girl, you so crazy," Ce-Ce says, playfully slapping Lenore's hand.

"Move over," Nadine says, "let me handle this." She takes hold of the door and Lenore sits down. When a woman comes in, Nadine holds out her hand. The woman heads toward the third stall, trying to ignore Nadine.

"That one's out of order too," she says. "Mr. Smith said for me to collect money on this one 'cause the door's acting funny."

"Who's Mr. Smith?" This makes me cringe. What if we are found out? Will they call the police and have us locked up?

81

"He's the manager," Nadine says, lying through her teeth.

"I thought his name was Gilbertson," the woman says.

"Oh, Mr. Gilbertson, he's the owner. Mr. Smith, he's the manager. He asked us to do this until he comes back."

The woman hands over her dime. When she leaves, we are all relieved, but in seconds there is a long line. Soon no one even asks what we're doing. They just hand their dimes over to Nadine, and she stuffs the money in her pocket.

After about twenty-six people have come through, we run out of the bathroom and line up at the refreshment counter. We have enough money for drinks, pizza, fries, popcorn, and Jujubees. We cart it all back to our seats and stuff ourselves.

"That sure was good," Ce-Ce says, wiping pizza sauce from around her mouth.

"Yeah," Nadine says, "sure was." She laughs, pushing and shoving us.

We all pat Lenore's back. "Good thinking, Lenore," I say. She smiles and winks.

The organ is beckoning. We roll back out onto

the floor. Pretty soon we have a little routine going with our hands and feet. We dip our hips and swivel our shoulders and even learn to do crossovers. We have our arms linked over each other's shoulders, chorus-line style. *Step, step. Swivel, swivel. Step, step. Dip, dip. Step, step, cross over, cross over.*

I could do this for hours. Gliding and rolling. Then Lenore looks at her watch and says, "Oops! It's nearly four thirty. We've got to go!"

I am still trying to get the hang of stopping. I dig my whole left toe into the wood floor and scoot out of the rail opening. The music stops, and we turn in our skates and retrieve our shoes. In our socks we hunt for our seats to put our stuff back on. Ce-Ce knocks me on the shoulder putting on her red parka. Nadine slaps me in the face with her purple scarf.

"Sorry."

"Sorry."

We all laugh and get carried out on a wave of people heading for the exits.

Mrs. Robinson is waiting in her car. She lets us listen to the radio, and we sing songs all the way home, Lenore with her arm around my shoulder.

. . .

Tonight as I lie in bed with Angela the Covers Hog, I think about how my trip to the roller rink will really give her something to squirm about. A lot of kids have never been anywhere like a skating rink. Kids like Artemesia. I wonder what happened to her?

9

THIEF

Mrs. Mumby's front porch has stuff piled on it like a raggedy old moving truck. Boxes. Furniture stacked every which way. A broken chair. A garden statue with the head missing. And pots, pots, pots with plastic flowers so that even in winter, that porch is magnificently in bloom.

Lenore, Nadine, Ce-Ce, and I are walking down the street, and Lenore says, "I bet you won't go snatch one of those dumb old flowers."

I know she is not talking to me because I don't want anything to do with Mrs. Mumby. So I chuckle to myself, but I don't even look up.

"Who, me?" says Nadine, cocking her head.

"Yeah, you," Lenore says. "You always talking like you so big and bad. Talking about how you're going to snatch Mrs. Harris's wig when she's in the choir room, changing into her robe."

Nadine sucks her teeth. "Girl, picking a flower

ain't about nothing," she says, putting her hand on her hip and snapping her fingers.

"Well, let me see you do it, then."

Nadine looks both ways, crosses the street, then sneaks up to Mrs. Mumby's porch and snatches a flower out of a pot and runs back.

"Girl, you so crazy," Lenore says, laughing. It is funny. One minute the flower is there; the next, it isn't.

"Yeah, it's about time for geraniums to be out of season," Ce-Ce says. "You know, I'm bored of them myself." Ce-Ce keeps looking across the street. Finally, she gets up the nerve and crosses over. First, she stops on the side of the house. Then she jumps up to reach the porch pots and grabs all the flowers in one pot at once. It is like the cartoon where Bugs Bunny pulls the carrot tops below ground and they all disappear. Then she takes them and throws the flowers under the porch.

"Aww!" Nadine says when Ce-Ce returns. "You're a bad girl!"

Then everybody starts looking at me. You know, Mrs. Mumby *has* caused me my share of troubles. She's always watching me. Opening her big mouth and snitching. I ought to race across and grab a flower for every wrong she's done me. Would serve her right. But even though I can picture that scrawny little four-eyed woman, her lips flying with gossip, something holds me back.

"Go on, Pearl," Lenore says, shoving me.

It comes down to this: I don't want to seem like a stick-in-the-mud. I suck in my breath and walk slowly across the street, pulling my collar up to hide my face.

"Hurry," Nadine says, "before she sees us."

I move forward faster. When I reach up to grab some flowers, the pot comes tumbling down too and breaks into a zillion pieces, spilling dirt all over my shoes. Then I hear the front door screech open, and when Mrs. Mumby calls, "What are you all doing?" from inside the house, I dive under the hedge. I can see the legs of Lenore, Nadine, and Ce-Ce take off running down the street.

Mrs. Mumby stomps around on the porch. "Scat! Get away from here, you rascals. Oh, Lord, look what they've done. My flowers. Why would anybody mess with my flowers?" Mrs. Mumby says to herself. She comes down her stairs and hobbles along her driveway. I can see the hem of her housecoat and her black wedgy shoes.

"Don't you all come round here anymore," she

says to no one. "I ought to call the law on you. This is trespassing, you know!"

The police? *Please don't call the police, Mrs. Mumby,* I pray. I hold on to the branches of the hedge to keep them from scratching my face. My knees are beginning to sting from the sharp rocks digging into my skin.

Mrs. Mumby comes over to the broken pot in her front yard. "Look at this mess," she says. "Lord, what is the world coming to? I can't clean this up. I got arthritis so bad. Lord have mercy." When she goes back up her porch stairs, she passes close enough for me to touch her.

For a while I can hear her walking around on her porch. Then it is silent. *What is she doing up there?* I wonder. *Sitting?* I need to change positions. My legs and arms are aching. My neck is stiff.

It seems like hours before I hear the front door open and close. I wait a few minutes until I'm sure that she is back inside. I know she will be watching the front of her house like a hawk, so I crawl around to the side, through her backyard, past the little garage in back that she rents out, and down the alley before I stand up to run home.

Lenore and the others are long gone. What if I

had gotten caught? That would have been rotten. Lenore is the first real friend I've ever had. I guess she couldn't help running off.

FLY ME TO THE MOON

The moon is 240,000 miles away. The sun is farther— 93 million.

The next night I am lying on my bed staring at the white face of the moon, all pocked and chipped like a giant cookie. (The one I didn't have after dinner because I didn't get dessert.)

I mean, how do they know that the moon isn't 241,000 miles away? Do they really have a measuring tape that long? Who holds the other end? The one on the moon? Even if there is a measuring tape that long, I know it isn't a person who holds it because no one's traveled to the moon yet. But President Kennedy says we have to put a man up there before the Russians do. I guess he doesn't want us to look stupid. And neither does our principal, Mrs. Carver.

Last winter she lugged her TV set into the auditorium and made the entire school watch John Glenn blast off into space. "That's Lieutenant Colonel Glenn, now," she said, pointing to a man dressed in a thick suit with a helmet that made it look like his head was stuck in a bubble. Two men escorted Colonel Glenn, and he got into a tiny capsule that sat on a huge rocket. When they lit that thing, it roared off, breaking free of the giant clamps that held it down, and thundered up toward heaven. "It takes forces many times more powerful than dynamite for the rocket to break free of Earth's gravity," the announcer said. "The main fuel tank is as powerful as a mini nuclear bomb," he added. And there was Colonel Glenn sitting on top.

"Who wants to go to the moon?" Mrs. Carver asked as we watched the rocket with Colonel Glenn inside get smaller and smaller until it was just a white speck about to be swallowed by the darkness of space.

"Me! Me!" Ray Armstrong said, jumping up and down. The rest of us weren't so sure, though.

"Ray, a smart boy like you could end up being the first Negro astronaut," Mrs. Carver said. She scanned the auditorium. "Students," she said, "the space program will be your ticket to a good job. They are spending millions of dollars down in Houston, hiring college graduates. If you don't want to end up as a janitor or a maid, you'd better study mathematics and science as hard as you can."

But what would you do up there all day by your-self? What would you eat? How would you get back to Earth?

The sheer curtains flutter. I pull the covers up around my neck. Even if I wanted to, I'm not going to the moon or even downstairs. I am grounded. It is eight o'clock, and everyone else is downstairs watching the end of the Disney movie on TV. But just when I think I can't stand it anymore, can't take another minute of being punished, I realize that being grounded in my room for throwing spitballs is not such a bad thing. I could have gotten caught for breaking Mrs. Mumby's flowerpot, and the police could have arrested me. I could be in prison, where I hear all they give you is water and bread and make you sleep on a cold hard floor, and there are rats and the ghosts of people who have died there.

It's funny how you think you are getting away with one thing, then you get punished for some-thing that isn't even your fault.

I mean, who looks out for innocent people? People like me who are just minding their own busi-ness and not bothering anybody.

I fired off one shot at Harold for pulling up my blouse at recess, and Mrs. Scott caught me. "If I see

91

you do that again, I'm going to send you to the principal's office," she said.

"Yes, ma'am," I said, and as soon as she turned her back and started writing on the blackboard again, I got whacked on the ear with a pencil eraser from clear across the room. There was Harold snickering in the corner and my face was getting red and I was so mad. He was kicking his legs up in the air, holding his stomach, and laughing silently behind his hand. *That's it*, I thought.

I had a good one going in my mouth, having chewed not one, but two pieces of paper into a spitting paste, and was about to pull it out and whack that boy good when Mrs. Scott asked, "What are you chewing, Pearl?"

I shoved the whole mass to one side of my mouth and said, "Thnuthin."

"Really? Let me see," she said. And I prayed, *Lord, help me to like spitballs* and swallowed. It went down hard, nearly choking me, it was so big.

I felt sick, but I managed to open my mouth. She must have seen a bit of paper on my teeth because off I went to the principal's office.

· · ·

Even as I lie here with a chilly breeze blowing through a small opening in the window, I can still feel the way my ears burned when Mrs. Carver called my mother on the telephone.

Angela comes upstairs, laughing and giggling. I can hear Mama with her, so I turn my back and pretend to be asleep. Mama helps her undress and put on a nightgown. I feel the bed jiggle when she hops in bed beside me. I can hear Mama covering her up, then giving her a kiss. Suddenly, the room is stuffy. I wish I *were* on the moon.

10

IN THE GARDEN

Hooray! It's finally warm enough to leave our jackets in the closet. I am so sick of mine, I could scream. The birds are making nests in the trees and bushes around our house. Some days you can hear them starting to twitter even before the sun rises.

That is the good news. The bad news is that though we Jordans live in the city, my father still thinks he lives on a farm. And where does he get workers? You guessed it. The only fun part was when we were in the dining room flipping through seed catalogs, staring at pictures that looked better than the real thing. And I don't even like vegetables.

All winter, packages arrived that fit in the palm of my hand. Some had seeds that were as fat as my thumb; others had seeds as tiny as a speck of dust. "Tomato," Daddy said, holding one speck in his hand. When I was small, I couldn't believe that a big fat tomato was in such a little bitty thing. Now it occurs to me that the fruit to come is asleep in the bud like an idea. First, it is a thought. One word, maybe two. They connect, and suddenly, more words connect, and you have an idea growing like a plant.

Last year's garden is covered with leaves and some dried-up old plants. There are also coffee grounds, eggshells, and vegetable peelings that I helped carry out here all winter. It is "D day," as Curtis calls it. "Ready, set, *dig*!" he says on this mild Saturday morning in April. We dig with hoes, shovels, and picks. Even Angela has to put down her dolls long enough to dig with a small trowel.

I might as well change my name to Pearl "Old MacDonald" Jordan. Today is hoeing and planting day. No wonder I've had a hard time making friends.

Daddy and Curtis bust up the big clods of dirt with hoes. While Mama and Diana rake it smooth and flat, Angela and I take a break. We lie on our backs in the grass playing "Guess What That Cloud Looks Like?" She is actually pretty good, seeing faces and animals. I expect her to start whining and complaining any minute about something or the other, but she doesn't. She is minding her p's and q's. Sunshine does a body good. I could lie here all day.

I have never been on an island, but I imagine that it is something like what our garden will be like when the plants are grown. By then many of them will come up to my shoulders, and it will be like having a jungle in the backyard. And there will be loads of vegetables hanging on the stalks. And we can just go pick them anytime we want to without having to see that slick-headed Mr. Norton at Swan's Market.

SLICED BREAD

". . . And get me some Roman Meal bread," Mama says, handing me a dollar bill. "That Wonder bread is too gummy."

"Okay," I say, putting down my history book.

"You can take your sister," she tells me, like that's a privilege. I am with her all day and all night unless I can weasel my way to Lenore's.

"Angela?"

"Yes. Now go on. And wait for the light at the corner."

I'm about to protest but think better of it. "Yes, ma'am," I say.

Angela, of course, has to take her doll. She bumps along behind me like a shadow, like we have all the time in the world. "Come on," I keep saying, and she speeds up a little. This is going to take forever.

Halfway there I see Artemesia and her sisters and brother in the street. At least she doesn't have on that yellow dress. Instead, she wears a black skirt and a white crepe blouse that looks too big for her. She still has on those same tennis shoes without socks, though.

"Hi," I say.

"Hi," she says.

"We're going to the store," Angela pipes up. "You want to go?"

Artemesia laughs. "Sure."

Angela is about the same height as the other little kids. They stare at each other.

"She's cute," Artemesia says.

"Oh, that's just my little sister," I answer.

"I'm not little," Angela says.

"Well, excuse me," I say, adding, "She's my *younger* sister."

We walk on. I can't think of what to say. "Have you seen that new monster movie?" I ask.

"No," Artemesia says. "We can't afford it."

"Oh," I say, feeling stupid.

Angela is busy showing off her doll. She lifts up

the doll's dress. "And these are her Sunday under-wear," she says. The little kids giggle.

We keep walking, past Nadine's house, past Miss Lela's flowers starting to grow up her trellis, past Lenore's street, past the corner where Mrs. Mumby lives.

The silence is killing me. "Have you heard the Little Stevie Wonder song 'Fingertips'?"

"No," she says.

(I am striking out with Artemesia, although there's something about her letting me know that behind those quiet eyes and those shabby clothes, she's thinking all the time—like she knows something that everybody else doesn't.)

"Boy, I'll be glad when school is out," I say, though I don't really mean it.

So I am glad when she says, "Not me."

"Really?" I ask.

"Yes. I like my teacher, Miss Webster. She gave me a journal for my drawings."

"Drawings?"

"Yes, I like to draw. Miss Webster said, 'Artemesia, one of these days I'm going to see your drawings hanging in a big museum.'"

"Wow!"

"Yep."

When we get to the park, Dink comes running across the ball field to the fence lining the sidewalk where we're walking. He starts shaking the metal fence like a lunatic. Artemesia gives me a puzzled look. But I decide that I'm not going to let this beady-eyed little jerk bother me. I ignore him as we pass. He shakes the fence harder. "Hey! Hey!"

Artemesia laughs.

"Hey! My cousin is in town and she's big!" he says.

"So?" I say calmly.

"I bet she can beat you up. Matter of fact, I know she can beat you up. She's bigger than you."

Angela grabs my hand. Good grief. First Dink, now his cousin.

"She's at my house now. I'm going to get her," he says, and starts running back to his house.

I look at Artemesia. She shrugs, but we pick up the pace.

Artemesia follows me inside the store—first to the canned-food aisle to get tuna for tomorrow's lunch, next to get dish-washing liquid, then to get bread. I check the date to make sure it is fresh.

Artemesia is looking at the day-old bread, which

in this store could be three days old and counting. Tens cents a loaf. She picks one up and digs a dime out of her pocket.

On the way home Artemesia stops at the bus bench and sits her three little ones down. She opens the bread and gives each one of them a slice. They sit happily munching on the stale bread and smiling.

"Can I have some?" Angela asks.

"No," I say quickly. "I mean, no, that's for them, Angela. We have food at home."

"She can have a piece," Artemesia says, handing Angela a slice. "You want some?"

"No," I say. "I don't want to eat too much before dinner." I am hoping that Angela won't spit it out and complain. Thankfully, she sits down on the bench and munches away, swinging her legs back and forth with the others.

"Do you draw?" Artemesia asks.

"Yes," I tell her. "Maybe we could look at each other's drawings sometime."

"Okay," she says. I know I should be getting home to help set the table and finish my homework, but I want to linger. There is something quiet and calm about Artemesia. She is so sure of herself.

In spite of the way people tease her. But I have to go.

"What about tomorrow?" I ask.

"No," she says. I don't blame her for being stand-offish. The way I treated her last time. But she adds, "I have to work tomorrow."

"Work?"

"Yes, I help my mother clean houses," she says. "What about the day after?"

"Okay. But I don't know where you live."

"That's okay. I'll meet you at your place after school."

"All right. See ya."

"See ya."

11

WINK WINK

I can't help myself. The next day I am supposed to be going to the grocery store again. But I want to see the poster bed with the frilly lace canopy, the pink princess phone, the basketful of hair bows, the mirrored dresser tray arranged with nail polishes and perfumes, the stacks of magazines. So instead of going straight to the store to buy eggs—which Mama forgot to get after she finished getting Curtis ready for the high school band concert tonight—I sneak off to Lenore's.

"Girl, I've been thinking about you," Lenore says, pulling me into the kitchen.

"You have?"

"Of course, silly," Lenore says, slapping me playfully on the arm. "So, what'chu been up to, Pearl?"

"Nothing," I say. Rats, it slipped out so honestly. "What've you been doing?" I ask her, trying to cover up.

"Going crazy," Lenore says, rolling her eyes. She

leans back with her elbows on the kitchen counter and motions with her head. "Girl, today I was Betty Crocker's helper." I look over her shoulder. There on the counter is a frosted layer cake on a glass cake pedestal. It is a little one-sided, but the white icing looks fluffy and is covered with coconut and a few black dots.

"Today was like home ec class," Lenore continues. "It's my father's birthday and my mother insisted on making a cake."

I can't take my eyes off the cake, not because it looks yummy, but because of the black speckles. "What are those?" I ask.

"Those are supposed to be ants. You know, like at a picnic? My mother's sense of humor. They're really dried blueberries."

"Nice," I say.

"Are you kidding? Have you ever had one of my mother's cakes? If you think the ants are weird, imagine the rest of the cake. It's called 'Devil's Food Surprise.' It's made with shredded beets."

"Gosh." My mouth automatically twists up like I am sucking on a lemon.

Lenore nods her head in agreement. "Yep," she says. "Beets." Then she sits down at the kitchen table. I am about to sit too when I notice her school-books. She flips through her math book. I know she is hoping I will do her homework.

"I can't stay long," I say.

"Oh, darn," she says. "Just for a little while?"

I look at the clock on the wall. I don't want to get into any more trouble with my mother, and yet I still want to be friends with Lenore.

She changes the subject. "Well, maybe you can go to the movies with me tomorrow."

"Me?"

"Yes, you're my best friend."

Wow! I think.

"Today's my last day of punishment," she says, "and Nadine and Ce-Ce and I are going to the movies tomorrow night. Can you come?"

Why do things like this always happen to me? I can't possibly tell her that I am not allowed to go to the movies at night. So I say, "I'm broke. I didn't get my allowance for the last two weeks on account of spitballs. It's a long story."

"Oh," she says. Then she snaps her fingers. "I've got an idea. My mother keeps money in a jar in the top of the cabinet. I can borrow some."

"Well . . . I don't know."

"It's okay, I do it all the time. She's doing laundry in the basement. You stand in the doorway and let me know if she's coming upstairs."

"Well . . ." Before I can say anything else, Lenore has climbed up on the counter, shoving aside the cookie jar, the sugar and flour canisters, the mixer and the toaster. I get up and move the cake so she won't step on it, then guard the doorway. Standing on tippy-toe, Lenore opens the cabinet and roots around among the serving bowls and platters and pulls out a white pitcher.

She jams her hand inside and yanks out a fistful of dollars. *Wow!* I think. *That's enough money for all of us to go to the movies for six months.* She stuffs the money into her pocket. But instead of being delighted, I have a funny feeling. Isn't this like stealing? Even though it is her house, it isn't her money. It's her mother's.

"Lenore! Lenore!" her mother calls from the basement. I jerk around.

"Hurry," I whisper.

Lenore pushes the pitcher back onto the shelf, shoves the platters and the bowls back, holding onto the shelf with one hand and moving things around with the other.

"Lenore! I'm calling you. Bring me some more hangers." I think I hear Mrs. Robinson coming up the steps. I slip back inside the kitchen with my back against the wall beside the door. Just as Lenore jumps from the counter, knocking the cake onto the floor— causing a loud *crack*, the plate shattering into pieces and the cake toppling into a heap—Mrs. Robinson comes rushing down the hall and into the kitchen.

"Lenore!" she screams. At first, all the color drains from Lenore's face. "Lenore! What happened?" Mrs. Robinson asks. I cannot imagine what Mrs. Robinson will do to her. But I know she's always getting after her for one thing or another like, "Sit up straight" or "Walk like a lady" or "Do not use contractions." What punishment would she get this time?

Lenore stares at her mother. Then what she says next takes my breath away. "Pearl did it," she says.

"Pearl!" Mrs. Robinson says, swiveling around and pinning me against the wall with her icy stare. I look at Lenore, but she won't look at me. "Why, you inconsiderate . . ." I think she is going to slap me. I am so scared that tears begin to well up in my eyes. I try to bite my lower lip to keep it from quivering, but I can't. A whimper slips out, more for what

Lenore has just done than for what her mean mother has just said. Mrs. Robinson takes this as a sign of guilt when it is actually sheer pain in my heart.

"We were having cookies and she asked for a second one," Lenore says, still staring at her mother and refusing to look at me. "I told her I would get it, but she insisted. Poor Pearl. It wasn't her fault. She was just saying what a lovely cake it was and that she hadn't ever seen anything so beautiful."

Mrs. Robinson swivels back around to Lenore. "So it was an accident?"

"Of course it was an accident," Lenore says. "Pearl wouldn't do anything like that on purpose." She walks calmly over to me and hugs me. "I know you feel terrible about it, Pearl. We'll get it wiped up in no time." She winks at me, then turns to face her mother while still holding my shoulders. "Mother, Pearl is still shaking, she feels so bad. After we finish, I'll walk her partway home to cheer her up."

Then Mrs. Robinson begins to rub her hands and wrinkle her brow. "I guess I'll have to get to the bakery before it closes," she says. She looks at the clock. "Well, Lenore, can you take care of this and set the table?"

"Of course, Mother. You go on."

Mrs. Robinson grabs her car keys and rushes out

the door. As soon as the car pulls away, Lenore bursts out laughing. "Girl, that was close. Sorry 'bout that," she says, slapping her thigh. "But I couldn't stand the thought of being tied to this doghouse any longer. You all right?" she asks.

All this time I haven't uttered word one. "I guess," I say. She slaps me on the shoulder and laughs again. Then she grabs the paper towels. We use a whole roll to wipe up the cake.

"You just made my father's birthday a much better one," she says after we put the last of it in the wastebasket. She throws some silverware on the table, and we start out the door. She walks me partway to the grocery store and tells me that she has a secret.

"What?" I ask, still shaking from the lie.

"I think I can get us tickets to go on *Teenarama!*"

That is a soul dance show for teenagers, like *American Bandstand.* My sister's been trying to get on there for two years. You dance and meet all these stars, like Smokey Robinson and the Miracles and the Temptations. I am amazed. "Really?"

"Yeah. My cousin knows the MC, and he's going to let me know about an opening for us. You and me." She squeals in delight, then adds, "Don't tell anyone. They'll be so jealous. Well, I gotta go."

"All right," I say, and walk on. But instead of heading right back home, she goes to the park. Lenore is really something. I know better, so I go straight to get the eggs.

I still have a buzzing feeling in my ear, though, and keep rubbing at it all the way to the grocery store and all the way home. I need to talk to someone.

BUSY SIGNAL

Mama hasn't even come up for air. She barely acknowledges me coming home and putting the eggs in the refrigerator because she's surrounded by piles of paper on her desk. We are having leftovers, again. Curtis always asks how you can have leftovers if it originally came out of a can.

Diana has an economics project due. She has it spread out in the dining room, covering the table and floor. She is explaining the world banking system. She's searching for the scissors when I notice them under a sheet of paper on a chair. I get them and hand them to her.

"Thanks," she says. That is the nicest thing she has probably ever said to me.

"I like the way you cut the arrows out of construction paper," I say.

"Thanks," she says again, gluing typed pages on her poster board.

I want to ask her about Lenore. Instead, I say, "How's Connie?"

"What?"

"Your best friend, Connie?"

"All right, I guess," she mumbles.

"Does she ever do things that you think are strange?"

"What? Connie is not strange. What are you talking about?"

"Well, I know *she's* not strange, but—"

"Can't you see that I haven't got time to be bothered with you right now?"

While she is drawing a cutting line with a ruler, I try to think of another approach—to ask her if it's all right to take the blame for something that you didn't do—but Diana accidentally knocks over the rubber cement with the ruler. It just misses the poster. "See what you made me do? Mama! Call Pearl!"

"But I wasn't doing anything."

"Pearl!" Mama calls from the kitchen. So I leave. Lenore's not a bad person. It's her mother who makes her do these things.

12

GOD-GIVEN

The next afternoon the doorbell rings. It is Artemesia. Thank goodness she doesn't have on that yellow dress.

"Hi," I say.

"Hi," she says.

I look behind her. "Where are your sisters and brother?"

"Oh, they're home taking a nap. I don't take them everywhere I go, but just about," she says, smiling.

We stand there awkwardly in the doorway.

"You want to come in?"

"Sure."

We sit in the living room. She sits on one end of the couch. I sit on the other. I have some of my pictures on the coffee table. Mostly stuff on construction paper or even lined paper. I even have a few old coloring books in the pile with pages that I thought I colored very well. I have some crayons on the table in case she wants to draw.

Artemesia has just one book tucked under her arm.

"Wanna see my pictures?" I ask.

"Sure," she says.

I show her the one that I drew of an evergreen tree. "That's supposed to be snow dripping off the limbs," I say. Then I show her one of some flowers and one of a cat. "I kind of messed up on this one 'cause I don't have a cat. I drew it from a magazine."

I keep going. "This one is supposed to be our garden. That's a tomato."

"I like this one," she says. "It feels like you are inside of the garden when you look at it."

I show her a few pages in the coloring books. I was really proud of how I colored this girl holding a watering can. I had even colored her face light brown. "Even with a box of sixty-four crayons, you can't really get the color right," I say.

"I know," she says. "There's only one color for skin."

I pile my stuff back up and make room for hers. "Let's see yours," I say.

"Okay," she says, then adds a sort of apology, "Now, these are just sketches."

"Mine too," I say, but when she starts flipping through the pages, I can't believe my eyes.

"I like birds, as you can see," she says.

There are birds, birds like I have never seen—with designs on their feathers that remind me of Arabic letters that we studied in social studies class and geometric patterns that our math teacher has on a poster in her room. These birds look like they could breathe. Like the wings are flapping up and down and they could fly across my coffee table. The light shimmers on their feathers. They are painted in none of the colors in my crayon box.

Page after page. Birds in nests, birds in bushes, birds on fences. Then there are pictures of chairs and flowers and hats. But if you turn them sideways or upside down, they contain birds. Pictures within pictures.

Here are pictures of people. People working in fields, their skin dripping with sweat. People waiting for the bus, loaded down with old shopping bags. People playing music—guitars and harmonicas.

Children dancing, children doing everything. Page after page.

"I like children," she says.

"You did all this?" I ask.

"Yep. That's nothing. I have lots of these books filled up. Miss Webster buys me books and pencils and watercolors. I just learned to use charcoal, so those are not too good."

What do you say after you have seen something like this?

Mama comes in the front door with Angela. They had gone to the library. Angela has an armload of books.

Artemesia stands up, but with her head lowered.

"Who's your friend, Pearl?" Mama asks.

"Mama, this is Artemesia," I say.

Mama reaches her hand across the coffee table. "Good to meet you, Artemesia. You new to the neighborhood?"

"Yes, ma'am."

"Where're you from?"

"Originally?"

"Well, yes."

"Texas. But I've lived all over."

"Well, I hope you like this town."

"It's nice," Artemesia says.

Angela has plunked herself down on the floor and is already turning the pages in the sketchbook. "Look, Mama," she says.

"Oh!" Mama exclaims. She looks as Angela turns the pages, accidentally rumpling some. "Careful, Angela," Mama says. Mama looks, then peers up at Artemesia.

"These are just beautiful. You are extremely talented. Do you take lessons?"

"No, ma'am. I'm self-taught."

"Are you thinking of going to art school?"

"Well, I don't know. . . . That would cost a lot of money."

"Sweetie, these pictures are incredible. With your talent, surely you could get a scholarship. I have never seen anything as imaginative and original as this. This is exquisite."

Mama looks at my sad little pile. Thank heavens she doesn't say anything.

"Can I get you something—a soda or cookies and milk?"

Angela speaks up. "I want cookies and milk."

Artemesia laughs. "That's fine, thank you," she says.

"Well, let's go in the dining room 'cause you wouldn't want to spill anything on your work. Pearl, you help."

"Yes, ma'am," I say, and motion to Artemesia to come on.

We all sit at the dining-room table, nibbling little bits of our cookies and sipping milk. I try not to get crumbs all over myself and look like a little girl. I sit up straight and tall, keeping one hand in my lap.

Mama makes small talk and I listen.

"I had a great-uncle who lived in Texas. Ever hear of a man named Richard Williams?"

"No, ma'am."

"Well, Texas is a big place. I guess that was a silly question."

Angela leaves the table and comes back with a piece of paper and a blue crayon. "Can you teach me to draw?" she asks.

"Why, sure," Artemesia says, and lifts Angela onto her lap. She puts the crayon in Angela's hand and wraps her hand around Angela's and says, "Now close your eyes." Angela does. "What do you see?"

"A butterfly."

"Now open your eyes and draw."

Artemesia guides Angela's hand in broad strokes. "You have to be a butterfly while you're doing it."

They stroke the page with the blue crayon.

"When you get stuck, close your eyes again to see the butterfly."

Angela closes her eyes and they stroke some more.

"Look, Mama, I'm drawing!" Angela says.

There is a butterfly and a pear and a flower and a glass of water on a tablecloth. And if I had any doubt about whether Artemesia drew the sketches, I lay that aside as she patterns the table-cloth with designs that just flow out of the tip of the crayon.

Mama looks at Artemesia and says, "Amazing!"

Then Artemesia says she has to go, and we walk her to the door and Mama says, "Come anytime."

And I say, "Thanks for coming over," and walk her to the end of the porch, and just as she goes down the steps Lenore and Nadine and Ce-Ce pass by, going in the opposite direction.

"Hi, Pearl. Hi, Mrs. Jordan."

Artemesia walks up the street with her sketch-book tucked under her arm. She turns to wave once. Lenore and the other girls go down the street look-ing over their shoulders every two seconds.

"Well, that's a nice friend you've found," Mama says. "Someone like that comes along only once in a lifetime."

"Your friend," Mama had said. Can a friend be somebody that no one else likes but you?

S P R U N G

Everything has gone green. Not a sickly S&H-stamps green. A spring green that you will never see again until next year. Tender new leaves push out of the dirt in our garden. Even my hair is growing.

I go outside and sit in a lawn chair in the grass. Angela comes out with her cereal bowl. She is barefoot. She drags up another aluminum folding chair and sits beside me, twiddling her toes in the cool grass. We watch the garden like it is a TV show. Pea stalks climbing, cucumber vines beginning to run, carrot and beet tops getting bushy, thick bunches of lettuce opening like roses in bloom.

13

WHO'S THE FAIREST
OF THEM ALL?

In Sunday school Lenore whispers to me that she is having a makeup party on Friday afternoon after school. I can't believe it! As we pass notes back and forth about what we're going to wear, she tells me I need to do something about my hair. She says it makes me look like a little girl. Like I still need my mommy to tuck me in at night. She tells me I need a hair style that says "teenager."

MAKE OVER

I don't want to tell Lenore that except for birthdays, this is my first party. I grab a handful of 45 records, like I've seen Diana do when she's going to a friend's house, and scoot out the door.

Everybody is here, and we are popping our fingers and trying to sing harmony. Then we start pretending that we are at a beauty salon.

At first I was having the time of my life, then the next thing I knew, Lenore had chopped off my braid.

I was sitting in a chair in Lenore's bedroom with a towel wrapped around my shoulders as Lenore styled and restyled my hair while Nadine and Ce-Ce just cracked up. Lenore said all she was trying to do was get us (she had to tell Nadine and Ce-Ce when it slipped) on *Teenarama,* though you're supposed to be at least thirteen to try out. She said we had to look like TV stars.

It started like this:

First, Lenore was picking on Ce-Ce for wearing socks instead of nylons.

"Girl, my mother would kill me if I wore nylons anywhere but to church on Sundays," Ce-Ce said. "And I'd better take them right off as soon as I get home." Then she added, "Who you should be looking at is Pearl."

They all swiveled around and caught me in the glaring inspection spotlight. "I'm getting to her," Lenore said. "Pearl, you look like you're still in kindergarten." She walked around me, sizing me up like a watermelon or a Christmas tree. "You've got to join the sixties. This would be a 'Don't' in *Teen Magazine.*"

I didn't want to admit that I didn't even read *Teen Magazine*. Did they have it in the library? It wasn't near the history section or the novel section or . . .

"Yeah," said Nadine. "You look like a baby in those clothes. You make the rest of us look bad."

Ce-Ce nodded. "Uh-huh," she said. They all laughed. I had to laugh too. My mother was old-fashioned. She still dressed Angela and me in matching dresses for church.

"First off," Lenore said, "you got to get rid of those kneesocks."

"But my legs get cold."

Nadine rolled her eyes. "Well, at least push them down or something."

Lenore snapped her fingers. "That's it," she said, kneeling down. "We can bunch them around your ankles." She pulled my socks down and gathered them in folds.

"Yeah. That's better," she said. "Plus, it makes your legs look bigger."

My legs are stick skinny. "You think so?"

"*Ye-es,*" they all said in unison.

"Now you need to lose those sneakers and get some sling-back shoes. Some 'twenties.'"

"Yeah," Ce-Ce said, sticking out her foot to show

off her black leather sling-backs. "This is what the high school girls wear. They call them twenties 'cause they cost $19.99."

I tried to imagine talking to Mama about sling-backs when I had never even worn a pair of nylons. Then it occurred to me: How would I play basketball?

"And those jeans," Lenore said. "Don't you have anything else to wear?" I looked down at my pants. How would I ride my bike?

Ce-Ce clapped her hands together. "I know," she said. "Roll the bottoms up to make pedal pushers." Ce-Ce folded up the bottoms of my jeans. I thought I looked funny, but Nadine kept telling me that I looked sharp.

"No," Lenore said. "It's all wrong. The jeans have got to go." She headed to her closet stuffed with clothes and pulled out a tight skirt, though it wasn't tight when she got it on me. "You need some hips," she said as she looked at me.

"She can have some of mine," Nadine said, patting her butt.

Just when I was trying to step out of the skirt, Lenore stopped me. "But it still looks better than the jeans."

"Really?" I said as she pulled the skirt back up and rebuttoned it.

"I wouldn't lie to you," she said. "You look fourteen."

Fourteen. I hadn't thought past twelve. Maybe that's what was wrong with me. I needed to be thinking ahead. Thinking of myself as grown.

Then they all started primping in the mirror with Lenore's makeup. I watched Nadine use a little brush to cake her eyelashes with mascara. "You got something against makeup?" she asked, catching me studying her.

"No," I told her, knowing good and well that Mama didn't even allow Diana to wear makeup out of the house. Mama would stand at the front door with a box of tissues so Diana could wipe off her lipstick as she went off to school.

"Good," Nadine said. "You could use some color."

"Here," Lenore said.

"But my mama—"

Lenore cut me off. "Live a little. Your mama ain't here right now." She picked the brightest blue in her eye shadow case and greased my eyelids with it. Then she painted on some lipstick. I kind of liked the lipstick, though. It was a deep pink, about the color of a tulip. The eye shadow, foundation, rouge, highlighter, and eyeliner were too much, but the others kept oohing and aahing. A thought came to me: What would Artemesia think of all these colors in the makeup tray? But I said nothing. Bringing up Artemesia was definitely uncool.

The girls started combing one another's hair, and I sat on the bed. I felt so self-conscious, trying to sit down in Lenore's skirt and wondering how I would hang upside down from my knees in the apple tree. But this must be what it feels like to be grown up and doing what you want to do and having friends.

"Next!" Lenore said. I sat on the vanity seat and we all laughed. Lenore undid my top braid and my back braid and parted and reparted my hair, then she sectioned off a piece in the front and combed it across my forehead. She studied my face. "What you need is some bangs."

"No!" I said. I had never cut my hair before. "Besides, what's wrong with my hair?" I asked.

"Well, apart from needing bangs, let me ask you a question," Lenore began. "Do you know any movie stars—except Judy Garland in *The Wizard of Oz*—who wear braids?"

I hadn't thought about that.

"None, huh?" Lenore asked.

"I guess not," I said.

"Well, then you're not going to wear a braid all your life, right?"

"No, I guess not," I said again.

"So hold still," she said. "I want to make sure that I get it straight." I closed my eyes. She laid the scissors against my forehead and then just cut off the whole front section of my hair! "There!" she said. "Nadine, plug up my electric curlers."

I opened my eyes and looked in the mirror. One minute I was okay, thinking about how I had done something so grown up. The next minute, I couldn't breathe. I felt my stomach sink, and I needed to go to the bathroom. *Why did I do this?* I wondered. Now the front of my hair was stubby and sticking out. "Ahhh!" I screamed as if I had seen a ghost. I knew I was in trouble. I started crying, and they were hugging me and telling me that it was all right. They kept making me sit back down in the chair.

Then Nadine and Lenore curled and fluffed and teased my bangs and told me that I looked, "outta sight!"

"You really think so?" I asked, wiping my face.

"I told you I wouldn't lie," Lenore said. "You don't look like a little girl anymore."

125

They must know what they are doing, I thought. *They* do *look older than me. You're lucky,* I told myself, *to have someone to do things with. Someone who knows what to do, how to dress, how to style hair, who knows what's cool.*

At first I feel good walking home. People seem to notice me. I figure they think I'm some older chick who has moved into the neighborhood. Mrs. Mumby, thank goodness, is nowhere in sight. I see a light on in the shack in her backyard. Maybe she's back there getting ready for another tenant. Miss Lela is out working in her yard and doesn't even recognize me. I keep waving and she just stares.

Still, I'm not sure. I go in the front door, thinking I will slip upstairs so I can check myself out in my own mirror before anyone else sees me. But Curtis and Angela are watching cartoons on TV in the front room.

"What happened?" Curtis asks.

Angela jumps up and starts hollering, then Mama comes out of the kitchen and yells, "Pearl Jordan, what have you done to yourself?"

I have no idea how to get out of this. I had just started thinking about being fourteen, more than

126

two years from now, but I hadn't thought about the next ten minutes—the time it took me to walk home.

Curtis still has his mouth open; Angela is hollering; Diana comes downstairs to see what the fuss is all about and starts laughing.

"Pearl, I am talking to you," Mama says.

So I start explaining. ". . . And Lenore told me that I needed to stop dressing like a baby and that I needed some color and that I needed some bangs—"

Mama has her arms folded across her chest. "And if Lenore said you needed to jump off of a building, would you do that, too?"

"Of course not," I say. "I would never do anything silly like that."

"Well, you look pretty silly to me," Curtis says.

Mama gives him the eye. "Curtis, I am not talking to you. Go set the table."

"Yes, ma'am," he says, but he snickers and laughs silently behind Mama's back.

"And, young lady, I'll talk to you some more later. For now, go upstairs and take off those clothes. And while you're up there, wash your face, comb what's left of your hair, and come down for dinner."

• • •

HOW TO BE A LADY

Mama says we have to talk. She says she was hoping I would see that the girls I've been hanging out with have grown-up things on their minds. She sits down on my bed, tells me to sit up straight, button up my blouse, and wipe my nose.

"They're just developing faster than you are, sweetie," Mama says, rubbing my shoulders.

"Is something wrong with me, then?" I ask.

"No, sweetie. You're just where you're supposed to be."

"But I won't have anyone to do anything with."

"You've got two sisters and a brother."

"They don't ever want to do what I want to do."

"Well, what do you want to do?"

"I don't know." Then I start to whine and sniffle.

"What about Artemesia? She's a nice girl. Besides, I don't want you hanging out with that Lenore anymore until you're older."

I can see roller-skating, parties, and *Teenarama* evaporating right in front of my eyes. I cross my arms on my bony chest and start kicking the chair leg right in front of Mama.

"Pearl Louise Jordan, now don't press your luck," Mama says, standing up. "Quit banging that chair." I stop in a hurry, but big buckets of tears roll down my face and I flop all over the bed. So she says, "I guess I have to come back when you are more like yourself."

D O O D L E   B U G ,   D O O D L E   B U G

Do you know how many wads of paper it takes to fill up a wastebasket? Seventy-nine. I have practiced drawing all morning (I am banned to the bedroom for the weekend for letting Lenore cut my hair), and the only thing I have succeeded in doing is wasting all the paper that was supposed to last me until the end of school. No one will want to be friends with me now, not even Artemesia. I will never draw as well as she does. How can she do that? I am cursed. I have a big old sign on my forehead that says, ART: D-.

I find one more piece of paper and close my eyes and pray, then I open them and draw. It is a dinosaur, only I am trying to draw a cat. Why can't I do this? Artemesia made it look so simple. Why would she want to be friends with me? I can only draw stick people. I . . . I . . .

Does this mean that I am a failure?

14

THE GIFT

Auntie Gert has been down with a cold, and Mama has sent me over with food. But Auntie Gert says that what she really needs are some new crossword puzzle books and would I mind going over to Murphy's, the five-and-ten-cent store, and getting her some? I look at Auntie Gert's kitchen clock on the wall above the gas stove. The May choral concert at my school is tonight, and I don't want to miss it. If I hurry, I can run over to Murphy's, drop the books off back here, and get home in time to make it.

That's when I run into Artemesia. She is counting out change at the counter to buy stuff like lotion and deodorant.

"Oh, hi," she says.

"Hi," I say. Then I ask her if she's going to the school concert.

"No, I have to help my mother clean houses tonight." Artemesia usually shrugs things off with a smile, but this time she doesn't. She never seems to have fun. "I mean, I'd like to," she adds.

"Well, come on, then," I say, picking out two puzzle books. "We can go together."

"No, I can't," she insists. We leave the store. I walk Artemesia to the bus stop and keep on toward Auntie Gert's.

That's why I am so surprised to see her later. I have eaten dinner, changed clothes, and ridden over to school with Mama, Daddy, and Angela. Lenore is in the choir. Nadine and Ce-Ce are sitting in the very first row, right in front of where Lenore sits on the riser onstage. I know Mama doesn't want me to sit with them. I'm twisting around in my seat, looking for a way to escape sitting with my parents and Angela, when I see Artemesia walk in and stand against the back wall.

I pull on Mama's coat sleeve. "There's Artemesia," I say. "She's by herself."

Mama turns around. The only empty seats are near the back. Then she looks at me. "Well, do you want to sit with her to keep her company?" she asks.

"Sure," I say, bouncing up.

I squeeze down the row to the aisle and run to the back.

"Hi," I say. "I thought you weren't coming."

"I wasn't, but I talked my mother into letting me come. I told her that I would clean two houses on Saturday to make up for it," she says. "After all, today's my birthday."

"Wow!" I say. "So you're twelve years old already!"

"No, I'm thirteen," she says. I am confused. We are in the same grade, and surely someone as smart as Artemesia hasn't been held back. I think she can see me doing the arithmetic in my head, because she adds, "When you move around as much as I have, you miss a lot of schoolwork."

"Yeah, my mother said your family's probably in the military," I say.

"No," she says.

"But you said you've moved around a lot."

"We have."

"Where?"

"All kinds of places. Georgia, Arkansas, Florida, Michigan, Minnesota. Even California."

My mind lights up even as the houselights are going down. California. Florida. I have never seen a real palm tree, and as soon as I am old enough and have a job, I am going to take myself to places where there are tropical plants outdoors. But right now we need to take our seats. The choir is warming up, the pianist is practicing, and the janitor is testing the microphones.

After we scoot to our chairs, I whisper to Artemesia, "So how come you got to go to all those places?" thinking that maybe I can talk my family into traveling like that.

"Farmwork," she says.

"Farmwork?"

"Yeah, onions, green beans, bell peppers, strawberries, apples, grapes, you name it."

I can't picture what she means. Her father grows all those things and takes them to those places to sell them, and she gets to go too? "You get to travel with your father?"

"What?" she asks. But the principal has introduced the choir director, and the choir director has tapped her baton on the music stand in front of her, and the music begins.

"*'Tis the gift to be simple, 'tis the gift to be free,*
'Tis the gift to come down where we ought to be,
And when we find ourselves in the place just
  right,
'Twill be in the valley of love and delight. . . ."

There are some children playing instruments: a cymbal, a drum, a bell, and a flute. I settle back and listen. But all the while I am thinking about what Artemesia probably did in all those places. And how interesting it probably was.

> "Grab your coat and get your hat.
> Leave your worry on the doorstep.
> Just direct your feet
> To the sunny side of the street.
> Can't you hear a pitter pat?
> And that happy tune is your step
> Life can be so sweet
> On the sunny side of the street.
> I used to walk in the shade
> With those blues on parade
> But now I'm not afraid
> This rover's crossed over.
> If I never had a cent
> I'd be rich as Rockefeller
> Gold dust at my feet
> On the sunny side of the street!"

By the time the song ends, I'm actually swinging in my seat. The choir sings some show tunes and spirituals, then it is intermission. I can't wait for the punch and cookies, but it's a mob scene at the refreshments table in the outside hall. I know Artemesia is too shy to muscle her way through, so I grab her arm. They have every kind of cookie you can think of, which is why most of the boys are there, including Dink. I steer clear of him. We get refreshments and stand near Nadine and Ce-Ce, but they ignore us (like it was my fault that Lenore chopped off my hair). I decide two can play that game—plus, I want to know how Artemesia got to do so much traveling when I haven't been hardly anywhere—so we go back to the auditorium.

"Your father has a garden and sells vegetables all over?" I ask.

"No," she says. "We *pick* vegetables and fruits. But my mother says we aren't going to do that anymore. It's hard work."

"I know all about that," I say. "That's all we do all summer."

"What do you know about farmwork?"

"My father's got a garden. It takes up almost our whole backyard."

Artemesia laughs. "I've seen your garden out back, but I'm talking about picking at big farms.

Most of them, I never saw where they began or where they ended. There were rows of crops for miles. We'd pick two months here and move, then two months there and move."

"Are you going to move again?"

"I hope not," she says. The lights flicker and people rush to take their seats. *Artemesia is just a kid like me,* I'm thinking. *Why does she work picking vegetables and cleaning houses? She's the only kid I know who works.* As I wonder about these things the second half of the program seems much shorter than the first.

> *"Oh, Shenandoah, I long to hear you.*
> *A-way, you rolling river. . . ."*

Then the concert ends with:

> *"A dream is a wish your heart makes*
> *When you're fast asleep*
> *In dreams you lose your heartaches*
> *Whatever you wish for, you keep.*
>
> *"Have faith in your dreams and someday*
> *Your rainbow will come smiling thru*
> *No matter how your heart is grieving*

If you keep on believing
The dream that you wish will come true."

We run into my family as we shuffle out through the crowd.

"Robert," Mama says to Daddy, "this is Artemesia."

"Hello," Daddy says. "I hear you're from Texas. That's mighty big country."

"Yes, Mr. Jordan, it is," Artemesia says.

"Mama, guess what?" I say, butting in. "Today's Artemesia's birthday!" I start to add that she is thirteen years old, but I decide it might embarrass Artemesia.

"Why, that's wonderful!" Mama says. "I hope you got to do something special."

"I did," Artemesia says.

DON'T KNOW MUCH
ABOUT HISTORY

We have slipped into mid-June. I rub my hand on my old fifth-grade desk for the last time as Mrs. Scott calls out our names for the year-end awards. Math, science, English, geography, spelling, academic challenge, attendance, and on down the stack of certificates. She gives out awards for the best weather predictors, pet attendants, playground equipment manager, hall leaders, cafeteria monitors, crossing guards.

Christina gets one for best handwriting. I get one for turning in every homework assignment. I'm surprised that instead of the mathematician award this year, I get a writer's award. Funny.

I look around the room at the walls that are empty now—our pictures and projects taken down.

I will miss Mrs. Scott. The bell rings and I hug her around the waist, my body limp and drained. Everybody else shoves past us to get out the door. They are screaming and flinging their empty book bags down the hall.

She wipes my face and pats my bangs that still stick out because they are too short. "Pearl, you'll like your new teacher," she says. "I know her very well. She's going to love having you as a student. You can always come back to my room to visit me."

"Really?"

"Yes."

I stare back over my shoulder at Mrs. Scott, her hair neatly pulled into a bun at the nape of her neck. She waves again, her legs crossed elegantly under her desk as she gathers up her papers, and I walk down the hall and get on the bus. While other kids are singing and throwing old papers and shoes out the window, I know that school is very important to me. I always feel big at school. Mrs. Scott always made me feel I could do anything.

15

WRONG MOVE

Mama comes to the back doorway after dinner that evening while we kids—and even Diana—are on the porch playing a mean game of checkers. It's all of us against Daddy, "The Checkers King," with pieces hopping, sliding, and rattling on the board as Daddy gloats, "Take that, Curtis Wesley Jordan! My beanie-head boy."

"Oh, see, see? Now you've gone and started talking about my head. And I know you're worried now. Uh-huh!" Curtis studies the board, his eyes dancing from one red square to one black one.

"Look!" Diana says, pointing to one of Curtis's pieces. "Oh, Curtis, you've got him now," she says, jumping up and down. She's trying to exact revenge for every time that Daddy has beaten her at checkers. Daddy is ruthless.

"Aha!" Curtis cries. "Aho! Ahee!" He dramatically wiggles his fingers over his piece, grabs it up, and begins jumping, making the checkers shiver with fright. "There!" he says, shaking hands with Diana. Angela and I actually hug.

I think someone has finally stomped Daddy in the dirt for winning all these years, even when we were little babies and would cry. No more Daddy saying, "I am *Mr.* Superman to you!" as we all tried to wrestle him afterward when we were little bitty kids, ending up in a frizzy-haired, itchy-skinned knot, with Daddy still standing, proclaiming victory. "I am the master!" he would say, bulking out his chest like a cartoon giant. Then Mama would say, "Honey, you're going to get them all wound up and they'll be awake all night."

But Daddy always has a trick up his sleeve. Just when Curtis least expects it, Daddy starts smiling. First, it is just a twinkle, like a werewolf must give when he first catches a child walking past his house. Then comes the full belly laugh, his shoulders moving up and down, the muscles in his neck rippling. When he throws back his head, howling, and you can see teeth that could grind your bones to pieces, you know you've been had.

"What?" Curtis says, staring at the board. "What?"

"Don't mind him," Diana says. "He's just bluffing. He couldn't move if his pants were on fire."

Daddy raises his hand and sweeps up his piece and—*blam! blam! blam! blam!*—wipes most of Curtis's pieces off the board and onto the porch floor. "I am the greatest!" he says, pounding the table. "I am the greatest!"

Curtis stares in disbelief. "What? I've been robbed! You cheated!"

And just as we're all about to jump Daddy and tickle him to death, we notice Mama standing in the doorway looking strange. It is a look between surprise and disbelief, and I wonder if someone has really died.

"What's wrong, Marilyn?" Daddy asks as Angela climbs onto his lap.

At first Mama doesn't say anything, and I hope it isn't anyone I know because I will have nightmares for days.

"You all right?" Daddy asks.

"Fine," she says finally. Then she holds up an envelope. "It's just that we got more of a tax refund than I thought."

"So how much did we get?" Daddy asks.

"Seven hundred dollars."

"Are you kidding?"

"No," she says. And instead of mobbing Daddy, we mob Mama.

"We're rich, we're rich!" Curtis says over and over.

But rather than buying Curtis his very own car (beside the fact that he's only fourteen), or buying Daddy that fishing boat he's always wanted, or buying me and Angela the bunk beds that we desperately need . . . Mama and Daddy decide to turn the catchall closet under the stairs that lead to the attic into a bedroom—no, make that a roomette—for Diana. It is tiny with a small window, but it will become Diana's very own private room.

All the junk is taken out of there, and wallboard is put up and painted, a border ordered, and curtains made. Diana's bed is moved, the dresser moved, the desk moved. And now Diana has her very own pad where she and her girlfriends can go and be together and talk and giggle and whisper and play her new radio with the door closed.

Then the water heater dies. Just quits. Won't heat another drop. And there is the electrical work for the new furnace. And Curtis breaks a window playing basketball in the house with Melon.

I can feel hurt pulling at the corners of my mouth

and sting welling in my eyes. I am stuck in a double bed with Angela. One day you are transported outside yourself because you are rich. The next day you are caged up again.

SCRATCHED

Mama moves our double bed to the center of the room and finds old tables that Angela and I can use on each side of the bed as nightstands. Auntie Gert gave us a lamp so we won't have to get up to turn out the ceiling light. She also gave us a white chest of drawers that got scratched real bad when Curtis and Daddy hauled it up our stairs. With Diana's dresser gone, there is no mirror in my room now, and I have to go to the bathroom every time I want to look at myself.

Mama says, "Pearl, I'm doing the best that I can. Put yourself in Diana's shoes. She's a teenager. But I'll keep my promise to get you and Angela separate beds."

My eyes run anyhow, and she says, "You are looking at this all wrong." And I wonder, *Does she think I am standing on my head?* Or maybe she thinks that I *should* be standing on my head. . . .

"Think about the future," Mama says. But the last time I thought about the future, it got me in trouble big time. I ended up banished to the bedroom, with no allowance for a week and stubby hair. Plus, Mama said I had to cool it with Lenore.

My only solace: the smallness of Diana's room. It used to be a closet, expanded only a bit up into the eaves. It's long and narrow with barely enough space to walk down the middle. There is just one small window, not the two large ones on either side of *my* room that pull the slightest cool breeze from one side to the other. So when summer's heat starts choking us around the throat, Diana will be in there sweating like a dog on a chain. And trying not to complain.

A wicked smile spreads across my face.

Mama gets tired of looking at the huge scratch on the side of our new dresser, so Daddy strips off all the white paint. That's when we find out that it was originally a beautiful cherry chest of drawers with brass handles and an inlay design in the shape of a bird. Mama says, "You never know what's under the surface sometimes till you scratch it."

BACKYARD BALLET

It's Friday night, and Mama says we can grill out. It is the warmest day yet.

Daddy and Curtis fire up the charcoal grill. Diana and Mama make hamburger patties and clean fish.

Angela and I make a pitcher of fresh lemonade.

Curtis puts the new radio out the kitchen window and sets it on a table in the backyard, the cord dangling over the hydrangea bushes. You can hear the sounds of music all over the neighborhood.

Here we are in the backyard, the red-and-white checkered tablecloth over the picnic table, sporting our Bermuda shorts and summer sandals. Daddy dances back and forth as he brings the cooked meat and fish to the table. "Anybody else want a hot dog?" he asks. "Ain't summer till you've had your first hot dog outside."

"Me! Me!" Curtis says.

I want all of this to last forever. The blue-blue sky, the shade slanting across the hydrangeas, the beads of water trickling down the sides of the glass lemonade pitcher, the rainbow pattern that the sun makes on my plate as it travels through the glass. Then a new hit by Jackie Wilson comes on the radio, and we are all singing "Baby Workout": *"Put your hands on your hip, and let your backbone slip. . . ."*

Diana gets up and does the Workout, shaking her hips, stepping back and forth and side to side, her body whipping like a snake.

"Go on, Diana," Mama says. "Girl, you got it." She claps her hands.

Then Diana grabs Mama's hand. "Come on, Mama," Diana says, "let me show you." She pulls Mama up and they line dance. Angela scrambles off the picnic bench and joins in.

"Work out, Angela!" Mama says. Then Daddy gets up and does some old crazy move, like he's afflicted. Curtis busts out laughing.

"What is that, Bobby?" Mama asks, trying not to crack up.

"You remember this," he says. "We used to call this 'the bop.'"

"No, I don't remember, honey. That must be something that you learned down in Orange County somewhere."

"Here, let me show you," he says, and grabs Mama, whirls her around, then kisses her.

As Angela covers her face the doorbell rings. "I'll get it!" I say, and I dance through the house, snapping my fingers.

It's Artemesia. She has her little sisters and brother around her knees.

"Hi," she says.

"Hi," I say.

Just then Mama comes up behind me. "Who is it, sweetie?" she asks. Then she sees Artemesia. "Hello!" Mama says. "Won't you come in?"

"Hello," she says. "I was just taking my brother and sisters for a walk and wondered if Pearl could come?"

All of a sudden I feel awkward because I am having a good time, and I don't know if Artemesia thinks it is corny to be having a party with your own family. So I stop snapping my fingers.

"Can I go?" I ask Mama.

"I have an idea," Mama says. "I was just about to serve dessert. You want to come on back and have some?" she adds, looking directly at the little kids.

"No thank you," Artemesia answers politely.

"We'd love to have you, really," Mama says. "Would you like some pound cake with fresh strawberries?" she asks the three little ones. They giggle and wiggle.

Artemesia looks at me. I say yes with my eyes, and she says, "Well, if you are sure that it's all right. They love strawberries."

"Good," Mama says.

Before they eat dessert, Mama insists that they all eat some "real food" first. And they do. Then she brings out the cake and fruit, and the little boy claps his hands. When we all laugh, he hides his face in Artemesia's skirt.

Though we're full as ticks, with strawberry stains around our mouths, the sugar begins to kick in and everybody is dancing again. Curtis hand dances with Diana, turning her this way and that, crossing his arms back and forth, and reeling her into his chest. He even dances with me and Artemesia. She seems to just float, her skirt circling out. When he turns her, she spins like a top—a ballerina. "Wow!" Mama says.

"Show me, show me," Diana says. "I always wanted to spin like that."

Artemesia is embarrassed. I can tell. She looks at me. "Go on," I say, because I'm glad that my family likes her and doesn't care that she has on clothes from the Goodwill and has short tightly curled hair and gold hoop earrings that Mama would normally say are only for gypsies. She has beautiful, white teeth against smooth, dark skin, which makes her look like a statue.

"Okay," she says, "when you turn, lift your shoulders and rise up on the balls of your feet like this." Diana does, but she wobbles a bit. I try too. "That's right," she says. We all spin. "Now imagine a string tied to the top of your head." We try again. Then Artemesia and I dance. Mama is dancing with Diana. Angela and Curtis dance with the little kids. And Daddy dances with the meat platter.

Then a song comes on the radio, "Ebb Tide." It's an old slow song, but it's as full as a magnolia bloom under a full moon. The little kids giggle, like they know a secret.

"What?" I ask.

"Oh, they want me to do a dance that I learned," Artemesia says.

"I want to learn a new dance," I say.

"It's not that kind of dance."

"Well, what kind is it?"

"Well . . . ," she says, and starts moving to the slow beat.

First up, then back. Then swirling around and folding down onto her knees. She sways like a weeping willow. Then she rises as if she is pulling herself up on an imaginary rope, her head back. She spins slowly, one leg up in back, one arm curled over her head. She takes baby steps backward as if running on a tightrope, stops and hangs almost in midair only to bend over and circle around again. She dissolves into a new move with a beat, not one in the song, but one that would go with it if it were there, and she looks like the African dancers I have seen on a National Geographic TV special. She is so limber that her body can bend and leap effortlessly into almost any shape.

She ends by slowly swaying back and forth, like water lapping at the beach. Mama claps and everybody joins in. "That was beautiful," Mama says. "Where did you learn to dance like that?"

"When I lived in New York."

"New York!" I say. I can't believe that Artemesia has lived in the place where I want to live.

"Where?" Mama asks.

"Oh, they had an after-school program at a dance studio. We learned modern dance." She gathers up her little ones. They are like leaves folding up around her, like she is a flower closing for the night. "Well, thanks for having us," she says. My mouth is still hanging open.

I walk Artemesia to the door. She says she has to get home and help her mother. But I am dying to know why she left New York City.

"Oh, I was there taking care of my older sister's children while she went to school. She was studying to be a dentist."

"But why didn't you stay?"

"When you're a picker, you can't stay in one place too long. Besides, I don't know which was harder: taking care of babies or picking apples."

Then I remember something that I have been wanting to ask Artemesia. "Where is your father?"

"He's still on the picking circuit. My mother got tired of it. We see him sometimes when he's passing through to another state. I miss him and his fried corn cakes."

She steps off the porch, taking up the hands of her sisters and brother. And she is gone into the night.

GRAVITY

Suddenly, I am wide awake. You know that feeling when you're sound asleep—floating in your own space on a raft in a blue pool on a sunny day—and then, one second later, you are awake, standing up almost? Though you aren't.

Thump. Angela has jolted me out of sleep with a swift kick to the leg. I am about to whack her when she whispers, "Pearl, can we fall off of the earth?"

I glance at the orange glow of the electric clock

on my night table. It is two o'clock in the morning. I am actually too tired to be angry. We got in bed late after our barbecue and Artemesia's unbelievable show. "Go back to sleep," I say.

But Angela thumps me again. "Pearl, can we fall off of the earth? I was having this dream that I was falling off the edge."

That does it. I sit up and say, "Maybe you can, but I can't."

Then she whispers. "Why can't you fall off?"

"Because the earth is round, and if you could walk from here to China and still kept going, you would end up right where you started. Right here."

She doesn't say anything, so I lie back down and assume that she is satisfied and that I can go back to sleep.

But she isn't. She is crying. "But I'm afraid that I will fall off."

I am tired. Too tired for all this. "Angela, don't worry. You won't fall off of the earth," I say. "Trust me." If I hurry, I can doze back to sleep before the sleep wears off.

"But I was falling and falling, me and Chatty Cathy."

"Angela, listen to me. You won't fall off because there is such a thing as gravity, and no matter how hard you try, you are stuck here. Got it?"

"Okay," she says, sniffling.

"Case closed," I say.

"Promise?" she asks.

"Promise."

"Pearl?"

"What now?"

"You know everything."

"I know."

16

FIBBING

The next day I am riding my bike (actually, Curtis's hand-me-down) when I see Lenore, Nadine, and Ce-Ce. They are going to the shopping center to buy some records. Mama has forbidden me to go to Lenore's. But she hasn't said anything about walking down the street with her. When I look up, we have walked as far as Mrs. Mumby's. Just my luck. She probably has one of her evil eyeballs on me right now.

"Your mother won't let you do anything," Lenore says when I tell her that I can't go to the shopping center.

"I know."

"You'll never get a chance to meet boys," she says.

"I know."

I go one more block with them to the gas station and stop. I want to be cool, but I don't have the courage today. As we say good-bye a bus pulls up, and Artemesia gets off with a woman in a shawl who has a scarf tied around her head and is wearing tennis shoes without laces. This must be her mother. They each have a shopping bag full of old stuff.

Artemesia looks at Lenore, then at me. Lenore is staring a hole through me, so I only manage a weak hello to Artemesia. Lenore gives her the once-over, laughs, and rolls her eyes, and I am embarrassed for Artemesia. I don't laugh. The woman walks on, Lenore begins leaving, and as Artemesia walks past me, she asks me if I want to ride bikes later, because she knows where she can borrow a bike.

I want to say yes. But Lenore has walked off only a few steps.

"Well," I say, "I have to go to my aunt's house this evening. Maybe tomorrow?"

Why did I do that? Auntie Gert is in Jamaica. As soon as her cold got better, she had me lugging her suitcases up from the basement. I'd much rather ride bikes than go to the shopping center or look for boys. I'd rather draw or learn modern dance or hear about New York.

What is wrong with me? I will try to find Artemesia later.

ARTEMIS

I feel all jangly. Like a scratched record that keeps skipping and playing the same section over and over. It is long days that do this to you. A week of braiding key chains, weaving pot holders, building Popsicle-stick houses, making daisy chains, beading belts, looping macramé key rings, gluing seashells onto barrettes, putting decals on bars of soap, painting by numbers. . . .

I have been at camp for a week in the basement of the old community center building. Today was the last day. Mama sent Angela and me there to get us out of her hair while she works. Meanwhile, girls from Connecticut get to go out West on *real* camping trips. They ride horses all day. They round up stray sheep on ranches, and they practice tricks like standing up in the saddle. Backward. While shooting arrows. Then they dive through flaming hoops. They go canoeing on a river, catch fish, and rescue a cute baby deer that's gotten separated from its mother; and at night they roast marshmallows around campfires. They sleep in tents and write letters home by flashlight, listening to the sounds of the night. Not me, though.

What am I going to do the rest of the summer—

July and August—without being able to do things with Lenore?

To cheer myself up, I have gone back to the encyclopedia in my room. I'm up to "M." I would draw, but the fun has gone out of it. I do not think I will be an artist now and wear all black with a beret and sunglasses, even at night, and move to a little bitty apartment in New York.

Mama says a person the likes of Artemesia comes along only once in a blue moon. I hope she still wants to be friends with me even though I can't draw. I'm not such a bad dancer, though. Am I? I could show those people on *Teenarama* a thing or two—the mashed potato, the Watusi.

Lenore can't stand Artemesia. But she's right about a lot of things: I do get treated like a baby all the time. Didn't I have to drag the encyclopedia I was reading upstairs because I have go to bed at nine o'clock even though it is still light outside?

I turn the page. The moon is the second brightest object in the sky after the sun. It takes 27⅓ days for the moon to make one complete orbit around the earth. The moon has no atmosphere and therefore has nothing to protect it from meteorite impacts. So it is covered with craters large and small. The moon gets its light from the sun. The same side always faces earth, but we see different amounts of the sunlit area as the moon travels around the earth at different angles. These are called "phases." The cycle starts with the new moon, moves to the first quarter, then the full moon, and ends with the waning crescent.

"Turn out the light and go to sleep!" Mama yells from down the hall in her bedroom. "It's almost twelve o'clock. Your father has to go to work in the morning."

I look up at the clock on the table. Can it be that late? Angela is asleep beside me. I want to keep reading. I have lost my place. I'll just finish up this entry. I look down. The moon has been called many names, including Luna by the Romans and Selene and Artemis by the Greeks. . . .

"Pearl, did you hear me?" Mama calls. "You won't want to get up tomorrow. Don't make me come down there!"

I slam the book closed, reach over and turn out the light, and lie back on the bed. Art. Artemis. Artemesia.

• • •

THE FIGHT

Have you ever seen sparrows chase a hawk? It is not pretty. There was a sparrow's nest on the roof above the front porch in the spring. Every time I was on the porch, I could hear the babies peeping and the mama chattering away, telling me not to get too close. Like I could get up on the roof.

I was in the front yard collecting sticks for a dam that I had made where we get a little stream of water after if rains. Well, all of a sudden I saw a great big shadow swoop across the ground, and at first I thought that the mama sparrow had dive-bombed me. Then I thought, *That's an awfully big shadow for a sparrow.* I looked up. It was a hawk. He made a couple of dives toward the sparrow's nest, trying to chase off the mama and get him a baby chick or two. But the mama started squealing and squalling, and about five other sparrows appeared out of nowhere and chased that big old hawk back up in the sky. They kept circling him, pecking him, nipping him, and scratching him. A couple of times he even let out a cry, and I saw bits of his feathers floating down. Those little sparrows drove him higher and higher and farther and farther away from the house until they all looked like little specks. Then, one by one, the sparrows all flew back to their nests in my yard, and that big old hawk went off to lick his wounds.

Ever since that day I have stopped climbing up and inspecting birds' nests. I do not ever want anything like that happening to me.

I am lying on the floor in the front hallway, thinking about that, when the phone rings. I pick it up.

"What'chu been up to?" the voice says.

It's Lenore! She wants me to come over. She has another secret to tell me. I don't care about that so much as I want to learn any new dances or jump-rope rhymes she has picked up. I do not want Mama to know where I'm going, so I pretend to sweep the front porch. After a few minutes I pitch the broom in the hedge and steal away.

I'm not past the Dawsons' when I meet Dink coming up the street with a girl and two younger kids. The girl must be his cousin. I suck in my breath and try to look straight ahead. But I sneak little glances at her. She is taller and bigger than me. She stuffs her mouth from a bag of BonTon potato chips and drinks from a bottle of grape soda pop.

"That's her, Gee," Dink says to his cousin. "That's the girl I said you could beat up. You could sit on her and whip her. See how skinny she is?"

I stop. Honestly, Dink is gross.

Gee shoves Dink with one arm. "Boy, quit your foolishness."

I want to say, *Yeah, Dink, quit carrying on,* but Gee immediately turns her attention back to me.

She points to my pants. "What you got on?" she asks.

"Jeans," I say.

"You some kind of farmer or something?" she asks. Dink and the little kids laugh.

"No," I say, not knowing how else to answer.

"I thought only farmers wore jeans," she says. "You must be a farmer girl. You milk cows and all that stuff?" She snickers, showing bits of chewed potato chips stuck between her teeth.

"No," I say, though I don't want to open my mouth. I can't help myself.

"Well, you sure look like a dumb old farmer girl," she says.

Dumb? She doesn't even know me!

Then Dink butts in. "Go on, Gee, beat her up." He pushes her toward me.

"Quit!" Gee says to Dink, shoving him back. "Dink said you're going to beat me up."

162

"Me?" I ask, gulping.

"Yeah, you. But you better not bother me if you know what's good for you," she says, stabbing me in the shoulder on each word with a greasy finger.

I want to say, *Dink is full of it*. And while I'm at it, I want to say, *You better not bother me, either, chubbo. I can almost beat my brother at arm wrestling*. But I don't say anything. It is high noon. They walk east, and I walk west.

Mrs. Robinson won't let me in. She says that Lenore is on punishment and that Lenore is getting a smart mouth from hanging around me.

BUM RIDE

I can't find Artemesia. I haven't seen her in a week. She always seems to be somewhere, even though she is mostly by herself. She's probably looking for someone to play with.

"Stop being so jealous," Mama says. "I took you and Angela and Curtis to the Smithsonian yesterday. And last week to Great Falls."

At the Smithsonian there is this huge mastodon. You have to practically lie on your back to see the whole thing. It is dark in that room, and the mastodon seems like it is alive and could eat you up any minute.

Out front there is a bronze dinosaur that you can climb on. It's really neat.

So it isn't like I didn't enjoy the Smithsonian or Great Falls. It's just that I don't know why Diana gets to go with her friends to Coney Island, the world's best amusement park. And spend the night. In a New York City hotel. Mrs. Sanders, Connie's mother, is taking them. I haven't been to Coney Island in my whole life. I want to ride a roller coaster. I'm not scared.

I have begged Daddy to take me to Glen Echo, the little amusement park here. But it's for whites only, he says.

"Maybe they won't notice," I say. And he laughs. "Really, my skin isn't dark. We could sneak in," I say.

"Sweetheart," he says, and I'm thinking that I've talked him into it and I am planning what to wear in my head: my new pedal pushers with the bright pink butterflies and my white sleeveless blouse. "Come here," Daddy says, and I sit on his lap. "You know, you just made me realize that I should do something that I should've done a long time ago."

All right! In my head I am at that amusement park. We have passed it so many times on the highway.

"I'm going to write a letter to the folks at Glen Echo and to my congressman," he says.

"What?" I ask.

"I'm going to tell those people what I think. White people think they are better. But they are not. Everybody is the same."

I can't wait. Daddy gets up and heads off to the refrigerator, not to Mama's desk, where there are pens and paper. "When?" I ask.

He is eating leftover potato salad out of a plastic margarine tub. "Oh, I'll write the letter this week. I'll talk to Reverend Owens."

"So when can we go?" I ask.

"Oh, sweetie, things like this take a while."

"How long?"

"You might be grown by the time I get an answer. But at least it'll be a thorn in their side for a while for how they've treated people. And when we get that place integrated, you can look back and say you had a part in it."

Grown? I'll be old. Twenty-five years old. Thirty, even. Do people that old ride roller coasters?

This is not what I want. I'm just a kid. I just want

to walk up to that man at the ticket booth and say, *Please? Pretty please? Pretty please with ice cream on top?*

THE PLAN

"Girl, I been calling you!" Lenore says over the phone. I look around the corner from the hall into the kitchen. Mama is not working at the table.

"When?" I whisper, sitting down on the telephone seat in the hallway. I'm not supposed to go to Lenore's house, it is true, but Mama didn't say anything about talking to her on the phone.

"I've called lots of times, but I hang up when your mother answers. She sure is strict."

"Yeah, you've got that right," I say.

"My mother does a lot of woofing," Lenore says, "but she never does anything. Anyhow, guess what?"

"What?"

"There's gonna be a basketball game in the park tonight," she tells me. "Wanna come?"

Funny, Curtis hasn't mentioned it.

"Oh, I don't know."

"Don't be such a baby. Everybody's gonna be

166

there. There's gonna be music and everything. Don't you want to see?"

"The game?" I ask, because as much as I like basketball, it doesn't sound like as much fun as going to Coney Island. Or even Glen Echo, if they'd let me in.

"No, dummy, the boys!"

"Oh, yeah," I say. I don't want to seem like I'm not cool. I also don't want to ruin my chance of being a TV star on *Teenarama*.

"Okay, meet us at eight o'clock under the lamppost by the benches."

What have I agreed to? "How? My mother doesn't let me go to the park at night."

Lenore laughs. "Do I have to tell you everything? Tell her a lie."

17

THE LIE

I call Auntie Gert, who has just come back from Jamaica, to ask if she needs anything from the grocery. And I tell Mama that I have to take my aunt some bananas after dinner.

"Take your sister," Mama says.

"Do I have to?"

Angela is supposed to be grounded for breaking Mama's china doll. The one Mama's had since she was six. It was on top of the bookcase. Mama was angry when she saw it, like she had lost a part of herself, so she whacked Angela on the bottom. She must have been thinking about that because she says, "All right. But don't stay long." As I head upstairs to change I see that Curtis is watching a cowboy movie in the living room and Daddy is snoring on the couch.

I can't figure out what to wear. I mean, after all, it's just a basketball game. Lenore made it sound like a party. I still have Lenore's skirt from the night she cut my hair, but don't have the nerve to put it on. I roll it up and put it in a grocery sack, then dress in shorts, a blouse, and sandals instead of sneakers.

Auntie Gert nearly talks my head off about her trip to Jamaica. I sit on the divan, my legs pressed together like she taught me, my hands in my lap. She sits in her favorite Queen Anne wing chair, the top of her curler bonnet bobbing as she talks. Ordinarily, I love to hear about all her travels and about the "old" days, but I can't concentrate tonight.

"You all right?" she asks.

"Me? I'm fine."

"You mighty dressed up," she says.

"Just some old shorts and a top," I say. Actually, they aren't old. They're my best summer shorts, new this year.

"Well, they look nice. Time you stop wearing those blue jeans all the time."

I finally think I can escape and get up to leave, the sack under my arm.

"What's in the bag?" Auntie Gert asks as I am going out the door.

"Oh . . . it's . . . uh . . . Diana's cheerleading skirt.

169

I'm . . . dropping it off . . . at Miss Lela's to be hemmed."

"That's so sweet of you."

Now I've taken to lying.

BLUES

Streams ofcars easethroughthepark

Peoplewanderthisriverofdreams

Mandigs iceoutofcoolers

Themusicofcanspoppingbottlesclinkingdrinks

fizzingmotorsrevving

Womenwavelaughsnapclap

Theswingsarestill

The seesawhangingintheair

Bounce Bounce Bounce

Shoot Net Swish

Inbound Pass Bounce

Run Pass Rim Rebound Bank Net TWO!

I feel stupid hanging around the lamppost—
a wallflower hugging the edge of night. The place
where I've played in the day seems like somewhere
else tonight. A woman says, "Little girl, are you lost?"
I shake my head and look the other way. There are a

few kids running around, but most of them are with their parents. I try to make myself as thin as the post so I can hide in plain sight. *I don't know what I am doing out here,* I think. I can't believe Mama let me go to Auntie Gert's by myself. I cling to the sack under my arm like it is a life preserver. It never occurred to me that I wouldn't have a place to put the skirt on.

Someone taps me on the shoulder, and I nearly jump out of my skin.

"Girl! I been looking all over for you," Lenore says. "Where you been?"

"Right here. Right where you told me to meet you."

"Not this lamppost, silly. The one by the benches."

That lamppost is beside the courts. I couldn't have stood there right in the middle of things. "Oh," I say.

"Did you bring any money?" she asks.

"No."

"Goofy. Why not? We need to buy a drink."

"Drink?" I ask.

"A soda!" she says. "You know, walk around with something in our hands."

I am relieved. I follow her tight, short skirt and clingy sweater through the crowd. My sandals *clunk* every time her sling-backs *click*. I tuck the bag holding the skirt under my arm.

The air is humid with cigarette smoke, burning charcoal, and sweaty basketball players. Occasionally, there is a cloud of cologne. "How you doing?" Lenore says to some guys sipping beers. They grin and laugh. She switches her behind harder.

We finally find a guy selling sodas out of his car. "Two NEHI's, please," Lenore says. She gives me the grape and keeps the orange for herself. I start slugging mine down, but Lenore moves hers slowly up to her lips and sips. I get the hint when mine is half gone.

Heymanwhat'sgoingdown?
Ain'tnothingbutthe realthing,baby.
HeyMamayou sure lookfine.
  Comehereandtalktome. Whereyoufrom?
WelltheygotanymorelikeyouinPleasantValley?

Man!Didyouseethatshot?
  Heputthemoveonthatfella.
ThoseboysfromDowntownbetterwatchout.
TheseboysfromChurchStreetgoingto
  putahurtingonthem.

"Boo!" Nadine yells, and jumps up in our faces. Lenore staggers back and steps on my sandals.

"Girl, you scared me to death," she says, coughing out the words. "Where'd you come from?'

"My grandmother was watching me like a hawk," Nadine says. "I put my pajamas over my street clothes and lay in bed forever. Then I slipped out the window, took off my pajamas, and put them under Miss Lela's rosebush." I didn't think of that. "Don't let me forget them, hear?" she says.

"You so crazy," Lenore says, hugging Nadine. "Ain't you glad you came? There are some fine brothers here tonight. This is so much fun."

Nadine finally looks at me. "I can't believe you're here," she says. "It must gonna rain."

I want to say, *I'm not a baby. I'm through playing with dolls.* But I don't.

"What's in the bag?" Nadine asks.

"Uh ...," I begin. I don't want to admit that I didn't have the nerve to put on Lenore's skirt. "It's a ... old fabric scraps. I told my mother I was taking them to my aunt's so I could get out of the house."

"Oh," she says, unconvinced.

Teenageboysleaningagainstasouped
   upcarsmoking.

They croon, "You really got a hold on me . . .
You really . . ."

"Look! Look! Look!" Lenore says in a whisper.
We turn every which way. "No, behind me, silly."

"Which one!" Nadine asks.

"The one with the little mustache and the
Ban Lon shirt. See him? The one singing Smokey
Robinson's new song."

"You mean with the wavy hair and the long
eyelashes?'

"Yeah."

"Girl, he is cute!" Nadine says.

I'm starting to get the hang of this talk, so I
pipe up and say, "Yeah, he has a nice handkerchief."

"Handkerchief?" Lenore says.

"Did I say handkerchief? I meant teeth."

"Ohhh, he does have pretty teeth," Lenore says.

Then we catch a man staring at us.

Heygirlwhere'syourmama?Shouldn'tyou
beinbedsomewhere?
Hahahahahakneeslap
PsstPsstPsstHeylittlegirlcomehereaminute.

"Lenore, do you see that greasy old man over there calling you?" Nadine asks.

"Yeah, some crusty old fart," Lenore says.

When I look, a big old man in overalls with one strap hanging off his shoulder is looking at us and starts coming our way.

"Uh-oh," Lenore says. We scatter like chickens to another lamppost like we are playing tag.

"Girl, that was close," Lenore says. "We don't want some old bald-headed farmer like that."

"No way," Nadine says.

"Did you see those jeans?" Lenore asks. "Country-looking dude." We crack up. Then they look at me. I know Lenore is looking at my shorts and blouse. But she tries to look away.

"Well, what do you want to do now?" Nadine asks.

"We need to find Ce-Ce," Lenore says.

"Oh, she ain't coming," Nadine says. "Her mama found out."

Pssstpssst. Heywhat'syourname?
Wantsomecandy?
I got a nicecar. Wanttogoforaride?
PssstPssstHey!You!

"Oh, Lord, that greasy old farmer is coming again," Lenore says.

We scat, running to the other side of the basketball court. I'm having a hard time keeping the bag tucked up under my arm. I'm in a crowd of grownups who are mostly smoking and sipping from cups and bottles. "Excuse me. Excuse me," we say. I'm starting to get really nervous. Except for Lenore and Nadine, I don't recognize anyone.

"Dag," Lenore says. "I'm missing my chance." She jumps up, straining to see over the players to where the mustached teenager is crooning.

Nadine grabs her. "Quit. That man's going to see us. We have to wait until he's gone."

"No, I got a better idea," Lenore says.

Then I see Artemesia. *If Artemesia is out here, then it must be all right,* I think.

Lenore is spouting off her mouth about picking up bottle caps for ammunition.

"Pearl," she calls, "you coming?"

"I was just going to say hi to Artemesia." Lenore and Nadine would like her if they just got to know her. . . .

"Where?" Lenore asks.

"There."

"That creepy girl," Lenore says. "Look at her. Some old dirty trench coat. And that filthy yellow dress again."

"It's not filthy," I say.

"It is so," Lenore says. "Where does she get those nasty clothes? Does she do all her shopping in the Goodwill trash box?"

"You can see right through that dress," Nadine says. "And those run-down sneakers. They got holes in the sides." They both start laughing, slapping each other and falling around.

"I don't know why you like that raggedy-headed, ashy-legged, B.O.-smelling thang," Lenore says. "She probably wears the same drawers every day." They laugh harder. Lenore looks at me with pity. "You know, sometimes I wonder about you."

"That girl is just a dumb old creep!" Nadine says.

None of it is true. Artemesia doesn't smell. Her family can't afford things, but her clothes are clean. Her skin isn't ashy like they say. It is clear and smooth. And she isn't dumb. But I know I am not going to convince Lenore and Nadine. Not tonight. Artemesia sees me and waves. I wave back, but I am afraid to go over to her now. Do they think those things about me, too?

Lenore says, "Come on." She says for us to pick up beer and soda bottle caps and stuff them in our pockets to bean "Mr. Overalls."

The music is drumming along, the game is jumping, and people are betting and trash talking. We thread through the crowd.

Picking up bottle caps isn't the easiest thing with a skirt in a bag tucked under your arm. A couple of times I drop the bag and have to fumble around and go back and get it. The thing is getting awful crumpled. Even stepped on. I keep switching it from hand to hand, clutching it like a purse. Finally, I stuff it in the back of the waistband of my shorts, the way I have seen Curtis do with a baseball cap.

As I follow behind Lenore and Nadine, some boys are causing a fuss. Breaking bottles on the sidewalk. One of them is Dink. *Uh-oh*, I think. Gee must not be far away. I turn before he sees me. I don't want to get beat up.

Then I bump into Artemesia.

"Hi," she says.

"Hi."

"I was on my way back home from the drugstore and I saw you over here," she says. "My sister's got an earache and she's been crying all evening. It's hard taking care of them by myself. My mother's working."

"Is your sister going to be all right?" I ask.

"Yeah, she'll feel better when I put some drops in her ear and put a little cotton in it." She looks around, like she can't believe I am out this late in the evening.

"Where's your family?" she asks.

"I'm by myself. Well, not all by myself. I'm with them," I say, pointing to Nadine and Lenore scooping up bottle caps.

"Oh," she says. "I've been meaning to come by and tell you that I had a nice time at your house. But I haven't had a chance. When I'm not working, I'm watching my sisters and brother. I hardly have time to draw. Anyhow, thanks again for dinner. Your mother is so nice."

I am about to ask her to come over when she says, "There's something I want to tell you."

But before I can ask, I hear Lenore yell, "Pearl!" It is the way she says it, like a building is about to fall on my head. I spin around.

"Pearl, do you smell something?"

"What?"

"You know, B.O."

I am embarrassed. Nadine and Lenore crack up. I don't know what to do. I steal a quick glance at Artemesia. The sparkle has gone out of her eyes.

Then Nadine pinches her nose with her fingers and says, "Girl, I got some extra soap at my house that I can just let you have." They slap each other on the back.

Artemesia freezes. I want to say, *Shut up, Lenore. You don't know what you're talking about.* But I don't.

Then some boys run right between us, nearly knocking me down, and I hear firecrackers going off. *Poppoppoppoppoppoppoppop!* And we all run in different directions. Some people are cussing, others are fussing, kids are laughing. I am running back and forth, choking on smoke, and squeezing past people, looking for my friends, when Lenore and Nadine grab me and say, "Come on!" And I think we are just running away from the commotion, but they lead me to that big old greasy farmer. He is sitting on a chair with his back to us, and Lenore says, "Now!" And she and Nadine start throwing bottle caps at that fat man, who is trying to cover up his head with his arms. Then he whips around and comes after us. I stand in one spot until my feet figure out what to do.

He chases us and we scream, running through the crowd, across the basketball court with the game still going. Through the trees. Down the street. That fat old farmer finally gives up.

"Whew!" Nadine says. "I don't think I could have run another step."

We are gasping for air, bent over, our hands on our knees.

"Come on. Walk me as far as Miss Lela's," Nadine says. "I got to go."

"But I want to go back," Lenore says. "He won't bother us now. That fat-butted fool is probably in the gutter somewhere, dead of a heart attack."

"No," Nadine says. "This is pushing it. It's late. I've got to get back."

"Me too," I say.

"Oh, come on. Just a little bit longer. I didn't get his phone number," Lenore says.

Nadine runs up ahead and Lenore chases her. "Stay, please," she begs.

I catch up with Nadine, and Lenore chases me, too. We play this teasing cat-and-mouse game, shoving each other, knocking each other over, and playing tag for a block or two. Laughing and giggling. Then Lenore stops dead. At first I think she sees that dumpy old man. But she says, "Look, it's that funky girl. Let's get her."

They run up ahead, and in the light of the streetlamp I can see Artemesia wheel around when she hears the running footsteps. *They want to just tease her,* I think. But Lenore grabs that black trench coat and literally rips it off of Artemesia. Her package goes flying into the street, the small bottle of medicine popping like a bubble. I hope she doesn't take it the wrong way. It was an accident.

"Get away from me!" Artemesia says. Doesn't she see that it is just a game?

Then they shove her and pull on her dress. The bottom tears away from the top. What did Lenore go and do that for? I run up, but I stop. I don't want Artemesia to think that I am part of it. She will see that they are just playing and they will apologize and I will walk her home—wherever that is.

We all stand frozen like that for a minute. Then Artemesia takes off. Lenore and Nadine chase her through yards, between parked cars, down alleys, pulling at her clothes and pulling on her hair and stepping on the backs of her shoes and pelting her with bottle caps. When Lenore pulls Artemesia's dress up from behind, Artemesia scratches her across the arm.

"Ahhh!" Lenore screams. "I'll get you for that you black creep." And they chase Artemesia into Mrs. Mumby's yard, round and round.

When you are following, it's hard to get ahead. You go left and find yourself behind. I am doing all I can to keep up.

We run up onto Mrs. Mumby's porch, knocking over piles of junk, then jumping over the banister, into the yard, and up to the shack in the back that Mrs. Mumby rents out.

There must have been an old glass vase in the pile of junk. We all tumble through the broken bits beside the porch, rolling on the ground and scrambling to our feet. As I push off the grass, a pain sharp and biting goes through my hand. But I keep running.

Mrs. Mumby's back porch light comes on, and she is hollering, "What's going on out there?"

And Artemesia is inside the shack with her sisters and brother under a bare lightbulb suspended from the ceiling, and they are all hugging and crying. I can see them through the window, because the shade is up. I can see neat little mattresses on the floor and a small table with a tablecloth, a door with a nail where dresses and pants hang, her mother's shawl on a chair back, a cardboard box with assorted undershirts, and clean dishes stacked on a small shelf over the stove. An electric fan on the refrigerator swaying back and forth.

That yellow dress is stained with blotches of red. I don't know if the blood is mine, hers, or ours.

It is like fire, the pain that leaps from my hand. Bright orange, piercing the night.

I can hear footsteps thumping down Mrs. Mumby's back stairs. Lenore and Nadine pull on me. "Let's get out of here!" I look at them like I don't know who they are. I stand there, thoughts fighting inside of me, and in an instant I reach around for the bag with Lenore's skirt. I want to throw it in her face. It isn't there, and for a second I am horrified by this and wonder how I will pay for it. Then in the next second, as I look at Lenore and Nadine, I don't care. Just as they disappear into the night Mrs. Mumby comes into sight, and I look her square in the face and run.

OYSTER

I am an oyster. A thick, dumb shell. A clump of chalk, hard and clamped shut. Outside, I hear nothing, feel nothing. I am running home, but it is like moving through mud.

What is that smell—that cigarette, beer, sweat smell?

Inside, my body has gone soft and mushy, bound only by this shell. My thoughts are fishy.

What are you doing? Why did you do that? Don't do that. I did not say this.

"You are just like her."

I am not. I did not say this.

"She's your friend, isn't she?"

"Well, we're . . ." This I said.

"Isn't she?"

"She just comes over to . . ." I can't believe I said this.

"Isn't she your dirty little friend?"

"No! She's not." I said this.

18

GROUNDED

Now I am a potato chip. A thin slice of raw potato fried in deep fat and salted. While an oyster is soft and mushy, it is also considered a delicacy. Chips are snacks that just get gobbled up.

Daddy said, "Well, I see you decided that you want to spend the rest of the summer in your room. In a double bed. With Angela."

Mama started in on me. First, she said I had some explaining to do, but before I could open my mouth, she swatted my behind. "Who do you think you are?" Another whack. "Do you think you are a woman?" A whack on the back. "You want to be nobody?" Another swat on the butt. "I've got news for you, Little Miss Know-It-All. If you want to disrespect me and yourself, you will find life to be pretty ugly."

"Marilyn . . . ," my father said. I could hear, but I could not feel. Did not feel my feet touch the pavement as I ran home. Or my hand (my good one) touch the doorknob. "She is bleeding all over the carpet," Daddy said.

"I don't care if she bleeds enough to fill a bathtub," Mama said. "That was plain stupid. And to think that I trusted her. Told me that she was going to Auntie Gert's to take her some groceries. I knew I never should have let you go to that girl's house. She's too fast. Switching her behind up and down the street. Talking to boys. Calling boys on the telephone. Wearing makeup."

Mama grabbed my hand. The fire probably passed through it like a bullet, but I was numb. She dropped my hand, satisfied that I would live, and started again. "You're going to become a piece of furniture around here, sitting in one spot. But you won't be collecting dust. I have plenty of work for you. Your butt won't see the light of day for a long time. Don't even think about setting a foot outside, except to weed the garden. I'm watching you like a hawk."

"Marilyn . . . ," Daddy said.

"I'm not raising any streety children around here. Up in the faces of high school boys *and* men. Mrs. Mumby called and said you all are going to pay for the things you broke."

. . .

I once buried a grasshopper that I caught, then I dug it up to see if it was still alive. It wasn't. I poured water over it to try to fix it. I was six, and it seemed like that might work, might wake him up. I poked him with a stick. But he did not move. I felt awful. I thought about this as Daddy drove me to the emergency room. As a doctor stitched up the heel of my hand, I thought about the baby bird that I caught for my very own one time and put in a cage. Though I fed it ground-up worms, it lived only a day.

It is my writing hand. At first I thought I wouldn't have to worry about that until school starts. I thought about how I have another hand. A perfectly good one. But it is not my hand that hurts.

19

CINDER ELLIE

Curtis is making a circle around the kitchen table where Mama sits with her bookkeeping work.

"Curtis, what do you want?" Mama asks, finally exasperated.

I have my head buried in the oven, scraping off charred casserole and burnt baked beans and broiled bits of steak and fish. It's all sooty and gummy with the soap and water and Brillo that I'm using to scrub it out. The only thing that I can see well is the flash of yellow from my rubber gloves.

"Ain't we got something to eat around here?" Curtis asks.

Scrape. Scrape.

"Curtis, I have told you the word is not 'ain't,'" Mama says with a humph. "Besides, what are you talking about? You just had lunch."

"Yeah, peanut butter."

"Plenty of people would be happy to have peanut

butter," Mama tells him. "George Washington Carver invented peanut butter so poor colored children way down South would get enough protein."

I want to correct Mama, tell her the word is "Negro," but I am in the doghouse. The Cinder Ellie doghouse. Yesterday I defrosted the freezer until my hands were numb. Chipped ice with a pick and a small hammer.

"A punishment a day for two weeks," Daddy said. So I do not open my mouth.

"Well, we live up North, but thank goodness for Mr. Carver, because a boy would starve to death around here," Curtis says.

"Honestly, Curtis, fix yourself something else! I've got to get my work done," Mama says. "Do you have a hollow leg or something?"

"No, but I know someone with a hollow head!" Curtis taps me on the butt and chuckles.

I want to punch him. I want to smear the greasy mess from my sponge on his pants. I want to pour the pan of dirty water on his head. I do not move a muscle, though.

"Curtis, leave her alone. I've already made lunch for you all. Fix something for yourself and get out of the kitchen, please. Mr. Waterman is expecting me to turn this work in today."

I can hear Curtis rummaging in the pantry and the refrigerator. I can hear him opening and closing cabinets and drawers.

Scrape. Scrape.

Snicker. Snicker. Every chance he gets, he bumps into me and snickers. Getting the butter knife out of the silverware drawer. Bump. Putting bread in the toaster. Bump. Searching for the can opener in the gadget drawer. Bump. Snicker. Snicker.

Why do people pick on you when you're down? I can feel a ball roll up in my throat. I want to run away.

"Curtis, leave her alone," Mama says.

"I'm not doing anything," he says.

I want to trip him up. I want to get him on the floor in a full nelson. Until he begs me to stop. Until he—

I check my underarms. It isn't me. What has died and swollen up with rot in our kitchen? Something has fouled my air. Has kicked me while I'm down. Kicked me in the stomach. I stand up slowly and turn around. Curtis is standing at the counter chomping down on a second sandwich. Mama looks at me, then at him.

"Curtis!" Mama says. "Was that you? Because if it was, you need to excuse yourself!"

"What?" Curtis says, his mouth full. Egg salad.

Sardines. Liverwurst. Sauerkraut. I look at Curtis, mayonnaise around his mouth. "What?" he says again.

I want to throw up. I want everything to stop spinning, my stomach to stop hurting, my heart to stop aching. I want to run.

"Just where do you think you are going, miss?" Mama says as I head out of the kitchen. I pull off my rubber gloves as I rush to the back door. I wipe my hands on my jeans as I go down the back steps.

WHO'S THERE?

Mrs. Mumby is on her front porch when I run through her gate, alongside her house, and into her backyard.

"Hey! Hey!" she yells. But I keep running.

There is Artemesia's house, the little shack that had been turned into a small apartment. I've been so busy avoiding Mrs. Mumby that I didn't realize Artemesia lives out back. I bang on the door. No one answers. The shades are pulled down on the windows. I bang again. If she will just let me in, I can explain everything.

Bang. Bang. Bang. Why won't she let me in? Doesn't she know that I'm not like that? Bang. Bang. Bang.

"What are you doing?" Mrs. Mumby calls from behind me. I look over my shoulder. Mrs. Mumby is coming toward me fast. I start banging again.

"Artemesia! It's me, Pearl!"

I look back at Mrs. Mumby as I keep banging and trying to peek around the shade on the window. She comes as close as the rose of Sharon bush, then paces back and forth and points her gnarled witch fingers at me. "If you don't get away from there, I'm calling the police!"

Go on, call the police, I think. *I don't care. I have to talk to Artemesia.* I shake the door handle.

"You can knock all you want, but they're not there anymore," she says, crossing her arms on her chest.

I spin around. "What do you mean?"

"They've gone. Moved down South somewhere. Just picked up and left last night."

Gone? I feel sick, as if I have run too hard. I don't want to believe it and start rattling the doorknob again.

"Artemesia! Artemesia! Let me in! We can go for a walk. Or ride bikes . . ."

I feel a hand on my shoulder. "Pearl, they moved away," Mrs. Mumby says softly.

"Did she leave a message for me?"

"For you? Not that I know of."

I feel my shoulders roll forward along with my head. It's hard to hold it up.

"They didn't leave no message," Mrs. Mumby says. "They're migrant workers. Here today, gone tomorrow. That's why I make them pay their rent on the first of the month."

"Where did they go?"

"No telling. Wherever they need crops picked, I guess. They were nice people, though. Paid on time. The mother worked nearly twenty-four hours a day. Artemesia, she knew what to do—took care of those little ones."

Then it hits me. It is one thing to make a mistake. It's another to never get a chance to say you're sorry.

The wind has gone out of me. There I am in Mrs. Mumby's arms, crying like a baby.

"You used to be such a nice little girl," she says. "What happened to you? I knew your grandmother. She and I were the best of friends, ever since we were girls."

I did not know this. How could my grandmother have been friends with such a funny-looking, mean woman?

"If she saw the way you've been acting, she would turn over in her grave," Mrs. Mumby adds.

"Is . . . she . . . ever . . . coming . . . back?" I ask between sobs.

Mrs. Mumby looks at me strangely.

"Is . . . Artemesia . . . coming . . . back?"

"Oh," she says. "No, those people don't never go to the same place twice. Why do you want to see that girl?"

"I . . . need to . . . tell . . . her . . . some . . . thing," I say. I wipe my nose on my shirttail, and when a string of snot refuses to be wiped away, I bury my face in my shirt to wail, but sound won't come out. What I hear are footsteps pounding above the thrashing of my heart.

"Hello, Mrs. Mumby," I hear my mother say.

"Hello, Marilyn."

"Pearl! I've been looking all over for you! You know I have work to do. When I get through with you, you won't be able to sit on your hind parts for a week." Then Mama grabs my arm, but Mrs. Mumby pulls me back and shushes Mama.

"Marilyn, I know she's your daughter, but this isn't a good time for that right now," Mrs. Mumby says.

"But she is on punishment for—"

"I know. I'll send her back in a little while."

I look at Mama, then at Artemesia's empty apartment. My face is all snotty and my mouth twists open. But no words come out.

20

TEA PARTY

Mrs. Mumby has gone to her bedroom and taken off her housecoat and put on a shirtdress. She's even taken the curlers out of her hair. We sit at her kitchen table while she drinks iced tea. Water in an electric kettle simmers on the counter for another batch.

"Yes, I keep a jug of tea ready all the time," she says. "You never know when you'll need some to perk you up."

I say nothing. I stare at my glass, the water beads streaming down the sides.

"I know how you feel," she says. "First, I lost my sister. Then I lost my best friend when your grandmother died. She was like another sister to me. You were just a little bitty thing when she passed."

What did my grandmother see in Mrs. Mumby? She is funny-looking and has a junky house with stuff piled up everywhere. My grandmother was as neat as a pin and everybody said she was beautiful.

Mrs. Mumby finally gets up and starts in on a pile of dishes in the sink. She hums as she washes.

"Do you know how to brew a proper cup of tea?"

I do not care. I don't even know what I'm doing in Mrs. Mumby's house. In her kitchen. My face all puffed up from crying. But I know I am about to find out.

"Well, the secret to good tea is water."

I look up at her. My eyebrows knit together. *She must think I'm really stupid,* I think. She is going to try to get even with me by talking me to death.

"Did you know that?" she asks.

"No, ma'am," I say.

"I go out to my sister's old place, out in the country. A young family lives there now. My sister had a well—best water around. I bring home a few jugs."

I figure I'll drink my tea, then excuse myself. Go back to the house of torture. Take my next punishment. Listen to my mother answer the phone and say, *No, Pearl is not receiving phone calls, ever, thank you.*

Mrs. Mumby begins, "Now, you don't boil the water all rough like you're cooking potatoes. You bring it to a simmer, then cut it off real quick. Let it sit for a few seconds until it stops bubbling.

"Now, some people will dunk the tea bags right in the kettle or the pan of water. Well, that's what you do when you're washing clothes. But I put the tea bag in a cup and slowly and gently pour the water over the tea. This releases the oils and flavors, you see. You'll be able to smell the aroma of the tea.

"Then you let it sit for about two to three minutes. Let it calm down and do its thing. But whatever you do, don't squeeze the tea bag. That makes the tea bitter. It's always best to be gentle with things."

She rinses soap off two round cake pans, then dries her hands.

"Want some more tea?"

I want to say no. Here is my chance to scat. But I can't stop thinking about what she has said: "It's best to be gentle."

She takes my silence as a yes and refills my glass.

"Yes, your grandmother and I used to be best friends."

"Really?" I ask.

"Sure were. She would say, 'Hattie, why don't you go to the church picnic with me.' Or, 'Hattie, we're going to the beach, why don't you come?' We used to do everything together. Jump rope. Play beautician. Sew. Make snow angels.

"Even when we were adults and it would snow, she'd call me on the phone. 'Hattie,' she would say, 'I believe we got three to four inches of new snow.' 'All right, Carrie,' I'd say. 'I'll be right over after I get the children off to school.'

"I often wondered what it would be like if our children came home early and saw two grown women flapping their arms in the snow."

Imagine my grandmother and Mrs. Mumby lying in the snow making snow angels.

"'Course, it didn't start out that way." Mrs. Mumby laughs and shakes her head.

"What?" I ask.

"I didn't think your grandmother—or anybody else—would pay any attention to me. She was a beautiful girl. Tall and shapely with long, straight, pretty hair. I was a skinny little kid with fuzzy hair and knock-knees. I was a little bit bucktoothed, which I'm not anymore because I've got dentures. Didn't have braces in those days. And even if they did, we couldn't afford them.

"I thought, 'Now why would Carrie Mae want to be friends with me?'"

Artemesia? Can you hear me?

Mrs. Mumby drinks some tea, then says, "She

said, 'Hattie, remember when that mad dog was chasing us in the alley and I fell down?' And I said, 'How could I forget? That was some mean dog. Used to chase everybody.'"

Artemesia, wherever have you gone off to?

"She said, 'Everybody ran away but you. You came back and helped me up. And we got out of that alley where we weren't supposed to be in the first place.' I said, 'Sure did.' Then she said, 'You saved my life.' I hadn't thought of that. I just knew that we needed to get away from that vicious dog.

"Then she said, 'Hattie, I want you to do me a favor.' I said, 'What?' She said, 'I know you're self-conscious about your teeth. But ain't nothing you can do about it. You ought to just go ahead and smile.' She said, 'You're a real smart girl'—and I *was* a good student—'and you're kind, and I want you to be my friend.'"

Mrs. Mumby sips her tea, the ice clinking in the glass. I start to cry again and Mrs. Mumby pats me on the hand.

"I'll . . . pay . . . for the . . . pots and . . . vases," I say amid my sobs.

"It's all right," she says.

I think about Artemesia running, scared, her

clothes torn. Now I can never make it right. If I had just been like Mrs. Mumby.

"I didn't mean to," I say.

"I know," she says, and I wonder if she knows that I don't mean the pots and vases.

"I thought they were playing."

"I know," she says.

"Her dress got torn."

"I know."

Artemesia, I am sorry.

21

PICTURE THIS

"What's that?" Angela asks, looking at the picture in the small frame lying on our bed.

"It's a picture that Mrs. Mumby gave me." I shut the chest of drawers where I was putting away clothes and rub my hand on the inlaid bird on the drawer front. Angela is supposed to be helping, but her clothes are still piled in a heap on the bed. I am now the family's washerwoman. I can go no farther than the clothesline. Mama hollered at me some more for running off, even though Mrs. Mumby called and talked to her for a long time.

"Who is this?" Angela asks.

"It's Grandma and Mrs. Mumby."

"Grandma?"

"Yep. They were twelve years old," I tell her. "In a play at school."

"Grandma was twelve years old?"

"You probably don't remember her. She died right after you were born." I sit on the bed and fold more clothes.

"Do *you* remember her?" she asks.

"Of course. I remember riding the bus downtown with her and seeing the shops and cars and people. I would hold her hand as she went in the stores to do her shopping, and at the end of the day she would take me to the ice-cream parlor. I would stand on tippy-toe, trying to look in all the tubs of ice cream. The man would give me the biggest ice-cream cone I ever saw."

As I talk Angela moves closer and closer until she is sitting right beside me—our legs and hips touching—until she is almost on top of me.

"Did she take me to get ice cream too?"

I open my mouth, but something tells me to shut it. Something tells me that Angela would not understand. She had been an infant—too young to go on a bus trip to the ice-cream parlor. I cherish that memory. It's my secret.

I try to think of something so Angela can have a memory.

"Did I go with Grandma to get ice cream?" she asks again.

"Let me think," I say. "You know, I believe you did one time. I think so."

"Really?"

If I skip a few lines, it could be true. "You were just a baby. We got the ice cream"—me and Grandma. "Grandma sat you on her knee"—which could be true—"and let you lick the cone, and she would go, 'Bouncy! Bouncy! Bouncy!'"—which is what she used to say to me.

Angela jumps on my lap. "Show me!"

I bump her up and down, her plaits flying in the air. "Bouncy, bouncy, baby!" And I tweak her nose and tickle her belly for good effect.

"Grandma used to give me horsey rides on her knee?" Angela asks.

"Yes, all the time." (Which could have been true had she not gotten sick.) Angela hugs me around the neck. Then she slides down and starts folding her clothes and putting them away.

Oh, Grandma.
Where are you?
Can you hear me?
Grandma,
I'm the one

who took
your favorite
blouse
so I could
smell you
when I went
to sleep
at night.

22

MOVERS AND SHAKERS

I am supposed to be scrubbing out the kitchen trash can. Mold and mildew. Gray-green puffs of slime. Some of it gone pink. I cannot imagine anything more disgusting.

Curtis is having a field day, snickering behind his hand. The trash can normally is his job. Instead, he is watering Mama's rosebushes. Angela is on the back porch, playing with her dolls. When no one is looking, I ease through the backyard gate, onto the sidewalk, and down the street—even though Mama extends my punishment by a day each time I "run from" the house.

But I've got to check Artemesia's apartment for myself.

There is a man walking with a chair over his head. Two other men are loading a couch onto a truck in front of Mrs. Mumby's house. She is moving. Now I will never find Artemesia. I have driven away Mrs.

Mumby, too! When she comes out on the porch, tears are streaming down my face.

"Whatever is the matter?" she asks. "Did you hurt yourself?"

I shake my head no, my hair a big frizz ball all over my head. I finally open my mouth. "Why are you moving?" I ask.

"Moving?" She laughs. "Honey, I'm doing something I should've done a long time ago. In fact, you and your friends put me in mind to do it. I'm getting rid of all this old extra furniture and stuff. My mother's things, my sister's, my aunt's." She waves her arm around the porch and points inside her house. "This place had gotten all junky. It was a mistake to keep all this stuff. It looked terrible. I made up my mind that I just have to let go. I've got my memories. That's all I need."

I wipe my face on my arm. But I am standing there looking like a wet, orphaned dog.

"Looks like you could use some tea," she says.

I sip tea while Mrs. Mumby directs the movers, telling them which pieces to take—tables, rugs, lamps, cabinets. Then she asks me if I want to help bundle old magazines.

"Sure," I say. There are piles and piles of magazines: *Ebony, Jet, Look, National Geographic, Saturday Evening Post, Better Homes and Gardens.* They are stacked everywhere. I can see that this is going to take a while. As I tie twine around years of *Ebony*s, then haul them out to the porch, I keep looking at the little house in back where Artemesia used to stay. It is as empty as a cave.

When I go back inside, I ask, "Do you think they left their new address?"

Mrs. Mumby is sweeping a corner of the den where we have removed magazines, stopping every now and then to rub her swollen hands. She leans on the broom handle now. "No, honey. That place was pretty much cleaned out."

"But can we look?" I ask. "Maybe there is something with an address on it." I feel a little thread of hope when she nods her head yes.

Mrs. Mumby's hands don't work well with small tasks, so I use the key to unlock Artemesia's apartment. It is musty without the fan running. It sits quietly on top of the refrigerator. Our heels click hollow on the linoleum floor. There are a few cabinets and drawers. Empty. The shelf above the sink too.

One tiny bedroom no bigger than a closet is carved out of the small apartment. I wonder if Artemesia slept there. A double bed stripped of linens takes up most of the room. The rest is taken up by a chest of drawers. My glimmer of hope fades with each drawer I open and shut. As I walk back to the main room, I get an ache that a heating pad won't fix.

"If I hear from them, you'll be the first to know," Mrs. Mumby says. "Okay?"

"Okay," I say as I lock the door.

I can actually walk through Mrs. Mumby's living room now without bumping into anything. The front porch is cleared off except for two white chairs and a round table. She stands in the doorway when I leave. As I go down the steps, I tell her that I'll be back to help some more.

"I'll call your mother to make sure that it's all right," she says.

"That's fine," I say.

I'm walking to her gate when I look up and see Lenore and Ce-Ce coming down the street.

"Girl, where you been?" Lenore says. "I've been calling you." When I get out to the sidewalk, she whispers, "What you doing in that stanky old woman's house?"

"Yeah, looks like the garbage dump," Ce-Ce says.

Mrs. Mumby does not smell, and her house is not a garbage dump. I do not say this, of course. I look at Lenore and Ce-Ce, then walk away.

"What?" Lenore says.

"Hmm, she igged you," I hear Ce-Ce say. I keep walking.

HARBOR LIGHTS

The air is alive with lightning bugs. I watch the earthly stars twinkling against the blanket of night as I lie in bed, the moist breath of Angela's sleep on my arm.

I used to wonder, *How do they do that—make a part of their body glow on and off? And why? Is it a signal?* When I was little, I decided that they must have a tiny, tiny battery inside of them. I do not believe in Santa Claus anymore, but when I did, I thought this must be how Rudolph made his nose turn on too. Now I know that there is no Rudolph and that lightning bugs have no batteries. They have two chemicals inside their bodies that they can touch together to make their abdomens light up.

But I was right about one thing: It *is* the way they

talk. The males are saying, *Over here, over here!* to the females so they can attract a girlfriend.

Earlier Angela and I had caught a jar full—a living lantern, signaling in the river of night.

"I won't need a night-light now," she said.

"Why?" I asked.

"I'll put them in our bedroom."

This is not a good idea. They will suffer in the jar. "No, Angela," I said. "Let them go. I'll help you catch some more tomorrow night."

I expected her to whine and put up a fight, but surprisingly, she didn't.

"Okay," she said, and we poured the light back into the air.

Before that, though, before we went into the yard after supper, Mama called me over. She said she is trying to be patient with me. I am to stay away from Lenore, to not run off without permission, and to watch Angela for a few days while she gets some extra bookkeeping work done.

I am with Angela twenty-four hours a day; I think that is a huge sacrifice. Isn't she breathing on my arm right now? Won't she hog the bed later as she twists and turns in her sleep? But I don't protest. I am still in hot water.

Before even that, before my little talk with Mama—when I went to the grocery store to get her some celery for the potato salad that she made for dinner—I ran into heavyweight boxing champion Gee. She said she is going to beat me up for saying I was going to beat her up, and she shook her fist at me. Mama said I shouldn't worry about it, but I do.

23

PICKERS

Mama says if we want to eat, we'd better get out in the yard and pick. That goes for Diana, too.

"What about my nails?" Diana asks. Mama just points to the back door.

We get half-bushel baskets from the garage and pick, swatting at gnats and mosquitoes.

Cantaloupes and cauliflower.

Broccoli and beans.

Okra and squash.

Tomatoes and eggplant.

Zucchini and carrots.

Cucumbers and peppers.

Kale and corn.

It is hotter than the fireworks we saw several weeks ago, at only nine in the morning. Katydids are singing their sweaty drumming song. We pick for hours, filling basket after basket after basket.

Angela and I have on last year's old straw beach hats and long loose shirts to ward off the bugs. Curtis has on his cutoff jeans and an old undershirt. Diana has her hair knotted on top of her head, but it has mostly fallen down as she swats at bugs on her arms.

"When I grow up and leave home," Diana says, "I'm only having canned vegetables in my house. Or frozen ones."

Angela wanders. I am bent over on my knees, picking beans. The sun pricks the skin on my neck. If I think it is hot now, it will be hotter when Mama starts boiling water to put all of this stuff up for the winter. I'll feel like I'm walking on the sun.

"Look! Look!" Angela says, tugging on my shirt and nearly knocking me over.

"What?" I ask.

"A four-leaf clover. One. Two. Three. Four. See?"

Sure enough, it is. Angela runs in a circle, waving her arms and yelling, "Hot dog! Hot dog!"

"Let me see," Curtis says, snatching it from her.

"It's mine," Angela says, whining.

"Not anymore," Curtis says, holding it out of Angela's reach.

Angela starts screaming.

"What's going on out there?" Mama yells.

Angela screams louder, then runs into the house. She comes back with Mama, who goes straight up to Curtis, tells him off, and makes him give the four-leaf clover back to Angela.

"I was just playing," he says. "I was going to give it back." Mama rolls her eyes.

"You come with me, Angela," Mama says, and they go into the house. Angela turns around and sticks out her tongue.

As soon as they're gone, Curtis starts. "What a waste," he says. "She can have any wish she wants with a four-leaf clover."

Diana is throwing one bean at a time in her basket. "I know what I would wish for," she says.

"What?" Curtis asks.

"A normal family."

"That's dumb," he says. "I'm wishing for a car. The baddest, meanest, slickest car there ever was."

After all that talk he looks at me as if he's not really sure that's a good wish.

"What about you?" he asks.

I know what I would wish for. But I'm not telling. They wouldn't understand.

· · ·

I CAN FLY

I am a pink balloon. The sky is turquoise blue all around me as I float higher and higher. I cannot lie down. I have bounced from a trampoline into a giant tub of bubbles—all tickly and iridescent as I rise to the top.

"Mom, I can't believe it," I hear Angela say above the singing in my ears. She is rubbing her hands on the post of a white single bed. *Her* spanking-new white single bed with a ruffled comforter and matching dust ruffle scattered with pink cabbage roses. Mine is just like it on the other side of the room, a white nightstand just like Angela's sitting beside it.

Angela sits. But I cannot. She smoothes the comforter with her hands as if this is all a dream that she will awaken from and the old double bed will be back. I look at Mama, who is taking off her straw hat, the one she always wears to the National Zoo when we go. We just got home from the zoo, traipsing around all day, saving the best for last—the seals. It is like magic the way they fly around and around in the water. Though they don't seem to move a muscle, they glide swiftly over and under, leaping and splashing us.

We scream when the cold water hits our hot skin and dash back from the fence. But we run back to the fence over and over. It is our annual trip. Mama makes a picnic lunch, and we ride the bus the whole way to avoid the long lines in the parking lot. We get frozen custard for dessert and peanuts for the elephants and popcorn for the ducks. But Daddy could not go this year. He had something to do, though we begged him to come. And Diana had a "meeting" with the Rockets.

But this is what they did while we were gone—what Diana helped him with, though I thought she did not go because she is nearly sixteen and thinks she is too grown up for trips to the zoo. She leans against the wall, her hair covered by a curler net, her arms folded across her chest, smiling.

"Oh, Daddy," I say, and hug him around his thickening waist. I am all melty inside.

He lifts my chin. "Don't thank me, thank your mother," he says. "She managed to do extra work and take care of you kids too in order to buy this furniture."

I look at Mama through tears. I walk over and bury my face in her arms. "Thank you, Mama."

I am rocking back and forth with my arms

around Mama, knowing that there is something else I must do.

I hug Diana. She hugs me back. It is not hard at all.

POPPED

Mama says that Mrs. Mumby offered us a bedroom set that had twin beds. But she did not take it. It would have saved us a lot of money.

"But it was old and adult-looking," Mama says. "I wanted you to have something girlie."

I listen as I help her dry and put away the dishes, which I do without being asked.

Mama gets right down to work at the kitchen table with her bookkeeping as I empty the trash can. "Go on, Pearl," she says. "Check on your sister."

"Yes, ma'am," I answer.

Angela is making up her bed, copying me. She has been unusually cooperative since we got new beds. She is putting Chatty Cathy on her pillow in the middle of the bed.

Check. Thank goodness she's not into anything wrong. Now I can go about my business.

I am feeling more like myself, so I plan to do one of the experiments in the science book I got from the library. There are instructions for making a rocket. I am gathering up stuff while Angela brushes her other doll's hair.

"Do you want to draw?" she asks.

I have my head buried in the closet. "No," I say.

"Well, I want to draw," she says.

"Not now, Angela. Can't you see that I'm busy?"

I'm searching for the corks that I collected a while back. I had found a large soda bottle easily—though the Jordan children only get soda once a week because Mama believes it will rot our teeth. I am also searching for thin cardboard to make fins.

"Are you looking for paper and crayons to draw?"

"No," I say flatly.

"But I want to draw," Angela says, whining. "Artemesia would draw with me. Where is Artemesia?"

I stop fishing in the closet and plop down on the floor, my back against the wall.

"I'm going to look for Artemesia," Angela says. Suddenly, everything is ruined. "Where is she?"

"She isn't here," I say softly.

"Well, where is she? She's your friend. I don't have any friends. She was the best drawer. She was fun. Where is she?"

I can feel the bubbles bursting rapidly one by one.

"She's gone."

"Where? You're just saying that to be mean. You know where she is, but you won't tell me because I'm a better drawer than you. Where is she?"

I ran her away.

24

FORMING A PEARL

Daddy did not go to work today. Not because he is sick, but because he and Mama were up late last night, helping to cook dinner and make lunch boxes for two busloads of folks from down in South Carolina, where our minister's family is from. You could see kitchens lit all across our neighborhood while people were frying chicken and making sweet-potato pies for groups heading to Washington, D.C., to demonstrate.

Daddy explained this to us. He said we need to end segregation, right now. He said we need to end job discrimination. "We are doing this for you children, so you won't have to go through what we've been through," he said as he was making ham sandwiches.

"Yes," Mama added, "it's a shame that your father and I and our church members have to cook all this food and set up pallets on the floor at the church because Negroes can't go in restaurants and motels around here. It ought to be against the law."

"Yeah," Curtis said, drying pots and pans and handing them to me.

"Food?" Daddy said. "Being able to go where you want is nice, but we need equal pay. Negroes get paid half what whites get. Just give me my money, and I'll be able to eat where I want."

"You tell them, Daddy," Curtis said. "Can I go?" My ears perked up and I bounced around too. Maybe I'd get to go on what seemed like a giant picnic. It'd take my mind off things.

"Son, just because Negroes are coming to the nation's capital to speak their minds, the government has brought in all kinds of police and marshals and military. Like we're foreigners or troublemakers, when all we're trying to do is get the same rights as white people. No, I'm going with Reverend Owens along with other men from church. I believe one Jordan is enough."

Curtis slapped his thigh. "Dag." And I knew if Curtis wasn't going, there was no chance for me, so I went upstairs and read my new library book.

But this morning Curtis is gone too. Daddy changed his mind. Said Curtis needs to know what it's like to be a man and stand up for what's right.

All day Mama and my sisters are glued to the TV set, hoping to see Daddy and Curtis. For hours I watch shots of the crowds, choirs singing, and people making speeches. I can see it will take a miracle to see my father and brother in this mass of people, so I wander outside. It is quiet. Hardly any traffic. Like people have packed up and gone away.

I am bored. I shoot baskets, but I'm a little rusty and the ball keeps rimming out. So I get out my bicycle and ride up and down the street. I practice riding with no hands, shifting my body slightly to keep the bike in line. I practice riding ever so slowly and coming to a stop, but pumping the brakes back and forth so I don't have to put a foot down before I take off again. If you want to be good at something, you have to practice. On my way around the neighborhood—careful not to run into Gee—I see Artemesia's old apartment and wonder what she's doing on a day like today. Wherever she is. Maybe she's riding her bike. Then I remember the day that I lied when she asked if we could ride bikes together. Suddenly, I am hot.

I go back inside. Mama and Diana are hogging the sofa, and Angela is on the floor coloring. I stand in front of the fan in the living-room window. I can hear the TV chatter about the march. I go and lean beside Diana, my elbows on the sofa. "Wanna play checkers?" I ask.

"Shush," she says, her eyes fixed on the set. I plop down beside Angela and organize the crayons that she has dumped on the floor. Browns, pinks, reds, greens . . .

"Angela, let me have some paper—"

"Shush," Mama says. "Don't you know this is the Reverend Dr. Martin Luther King Jr. speaking?"

I know who he is. He is a man who goes around sticking his neck out for other folks, Daddy says. He is a big-chested, chocolate-colored man with a little mustache. In his speech he says slavery ended one hundred years ago, but Negroes are still "crippled by the manacle of segregation and the chains of discrimination."

"Mama, what's 'scrimination'?" Angela asks.

"That's when one person treats another person badly or unfairly," she whispers.

Dr. King stirs up the crowd like our minister does at church, his voice alternating between booming and mournful. Then he says the Negro is "an exile in his own land."

I know about exiles. We learned in Sunday school that the Jews were exiles when they were driven from Israel.

Dr. King talks about a lot of things, even his dreams. I lie down on the floor, watch the shadow of the fan flicker across the ceiling, and listen. In one of his dreams his children won't be judged by the color of their skin.

"Right on!" Diana says.

He says white children and black children ought to be able to play together. He talks about freedom, but a lot of what he says is a mystery to me. Grown-up and complicated. Like those Bible passages that are so hard to understand. But by the time he finishes, Mama is wiping her eyes. She is not herself again until nightfall, when our minister drops off Daddy and Curtis in the driveway.

It is hard to get Curtis off by himself because his head is so swollen from the adventure. He stands in the living room in his Sunday suit, running his mouth nonstop as he tugs on a pair of tennis shoes slung over his shoulder.

"What was it like, Curtis?" I get in edgewise.

"Lil sis, you wouldn't understand," he says, rubbing Angela's hair.

"Oh, Curtis," Mama says.

"Well, if you must know, I met some famous people. It started like this: Daddy told me I had to wear this suit and tie and I thought, 'Hmm, it's going to be hard walking that far in a pair of wing tips in this heat.' So I took my trusty black tennis shoes along. I figured that Daddy's bunions were going to be talking to him, but there was no reason why *I* had to suffer. Ain't that right, Daddy?"

"You're telling it, not me," Daddy says, loosening his tie and undoing the top button of his shirt.

"Anyhow, at just about Twelfth and Constitution, Daddy was doing all right, but the man he introduced me to—A. Philip Randolph—well, he got to talking about his feet. I had my sneakers in a little knapsack on my shoulder, because Daddy wouldn't let me put them on. Mr. Randolph kept talking, said his feet had gone bad from all the marches and protests he'd been in. So I offered him my shoes."

This part of the story makes Daddy roll his eyes. "Well," Curtis continued, "at first he refused. A little farther along he said, 'Besides, I got big feet.' 'Me too,' I said. 'Twelves.' Next thing I knew, he stopped on the curb, slipped off his shoes, and stepped into my All Stars. Ain't that right, Daddy?"

"That's a fact."

"Curtis!" Mama says, beaming and hugging my brother.

"We got pushed farther and farther behind him, and right before we got to the Lincoln Memorial, somebody handed me my black tennis shoes. I never did see Mr. Randolph again because only dignitaries could go behind the yellow lines. Daddy and I, we ended up way back down around the Reflecting Pool."

Then Curtis and Daddy look at each other and start chuckling.

"What?" Diana asks.

"Well, if I were you, I wouldn't go to the Reflecting Pool for a few days."

"Why?" I ask.

"Because Daddy took off his shoes and soaked his feet in the water!" Everybody laughs.

"Marilyn, we had been walking around for hours," Daddy explains. "You know I got bunions. Some people got all the way in because it was so hot."

"Anyhow," Curtis adds, "I'll never throw these shoes away."

"Why?" I ask.

"Lil sis, Mr. Randolph is famous. He told me that I could work for him after I go to college. Ain't that right, Daddy?"

"Sure did."

Everybody starts climbing the stairs. I am the last one, so I turn out the hall light. As I am getting dressed for bed, it is hard for me to be happy for Curtis. He probably won't ever let me forget that he got to go to the march with Daddy and meet someone famous. He will remind me every chance he gets, and it will be like a pebble in your shoe that you can't get rid of. Like a thorn in your sweater that you can't find. Or a splinter in your finger that you can't tease out.

Or like a bruise that is still tender. Like the little sting that still comes to me when I think of Artemesia.

ROOM #112

I wave at Mrs. Scott as I pass her in the hall with her new fifth-grade class. I sort of wiggle my fingers.

"Good morning, Pearl," she says quickly, and leads

her class away. I watch her until she is out of sight.

My new teacher is Mrs. Grace Taylor. She has her hair pulled back in a French twist. She wears a string of long pearls over a blue gray cashmere sweater.

"Good morning, Miss Jordan," she says. *Hmm, that's different,* I think. She must have read my mind, because she is scanning the class with a slow turn of her head as she says: "I will address all of you by your surnames. We are all young ladies and young gentlemen in the sixth grade. You must set an example for the younger pupils."

I take my seat. It's in the front but next to the window. Other students file in. Some I know, others I don't. Thank goodness Harold the Blouse-Puller and Eraser-Thrower is in another class.

I am surprised when Gee comes in and sits in the row beside me. Until then I hadn't paid any attention to the paper nameplate on her desk: GWENDOLYN PATTERSON. Believe it or not, she smiles, though I feel awkward. Through prayer, I have gotten rid of Harold only to find myself sitting beside Gee the Boxer. Geez.

During lunch she comes up to me. "I'm glad I know somebody here," she says, like we are best friends and she hasn't threatened to pummel me. I don't want to, but I make room for her at the table. After all, Mrs. Taylor is watching us with those perfectly arched eyebrows.

Thank goodness nobody's talking much during lunch. Normally, this would be a bummer, but today I am thankful. I pull out my red plaid metal lunch box and begin munching away at my celery sticks with peanut butter and my bologna sandwich. Gee's lunch box is pink and green with a mosaic of pony-tailed cheerleaders, pom-poms, megaphones, and placards that read, SUCCESS! and GO TEAM! and FIGHT! I expect her to pull out some barbecued ribs, but she has an orange cut into quarters, a tuna fish sandwich, and graham crackers.

We eat in silence until each person in our class has finished. Then we bolt out the door onto the tarmac, the boys on one side of the playground, the girls on the other. Gee clings to me like a shadow as I try to play hopscotch with some other girls. She tells me that her dad's been transferred here permanently with the army, they are no longer staying in Dink's house, and have moved up the street. She is glad to be out of his house because he was always starting something. And, "Oh, I'm so nervous to be in a new school." And, "Who is that girl over there?" And, "Do you think people will like me?" And, "They've got chorus here, don't they?" I am confused.

I wonder: *Is she going to sucker me in with kindness, then beat me up?*

25

LET IT GO

It is one of those crisp Saturday mornings in October when you know everything is going to change and there isn't a thing you can do about it.

I sit in the rocker on the front porch, my head pulled into the neck of my jacket, my hands drawn up in the sleeves, my knees tucked up under the bottom of the coat. I look out at the trees. Any day now all the leaves will be gone, the flowers will wilt, and the grass will turn brown. It's a shame summer has to come to this. Even the sun will kind of go away. It will be darker and darker when I go to school and night-dark when Daddy gets home. Soon there won't be enough light to play outside after school. There won't be much time to play outside at all.

A cloud of starlings rises up out of the nearly bare trees, fussing and fighting in the sky. The mourning doves peck at the ground in our front yard. They stay away from the starlings. *Go on! Go!*

Go! Go! That's what I imagine the doves saying. Every once in a while I hear a few robins asking: *What? What? What? What's going on?*

Sometimes the bird chatter is so loud, it's incredible; and other times the yard is so quiet, you don't know the birds are hiding in the trees until they take off. Boy, I used to wish that I could fly. But you know how you know there are things that you just can't do? Well, I know I can't fly. One time Curtis and I jumped off the shed roof over and over, using everything we could think of—cardboard wings, sheets, an umbrella, tree branches, the trash-can lid. As much as I tried and wished and hoped, I didn't end up doing anything but nearly killing myself. I sprained my ankle, and he busted his lip when he slipped.

There is something else that I still wish, though. I wish I had been a better friend to Artemesia. And as I watch the yellow maple leaves float down to the green grass, I let it go. If I get another chance, I promise I will be a better friend. A real friend.

Then I hear honking. Is it a flock of geese? I get up out of the rocker, walk off the front porch into the yard and out to the juniper trees that line the front beside the street, and look up. In a raggedy **V** shape, a flock of geese is flying south. Their long necks out, their long skinny legs back, their huge wings flapping. *Honk! Honk! Honk!* I want to run in the house and say, *Come look!* but the geese are going fast. So I follow them. Follow them down the street, cars whizzing past going in the opposite direction. I follow them until I can't see them anymore. When I finally look back down, I am at the park.

There are a couple of kids on the basketball court playing kickball. It looks like Nadine and Ce-Ce, having a great time. Nadine can kick a ball from here to kingdom come. For the first time in weeks I feel lighter. I run over to them.

Mama was right. I wasn't going to get beat up.

BIRD LEGS

Nadine and Ce-Ce hardly speak, but we don't need to talk. I just want to kick and run. I am on the opposite team and blasting away at the ball. A double, then a homer. My "team" is up 5 to 3 and playing to 11 when Dink shows up, causing a commotion. He jumps up in our faces, acting like a bloodthirsty mosquito.

"Hey, bird legs!" he calls to me.

Nadine and Ce-Ce laugh until he starts yapping at them.

"Girl, you sure got big ears," he says to Nadine.

"Boy, you better get out of here," she says, swinging at him.

"I'm not scared of you," he says, running off a little ways.

Then Gee arrives. "Hi, Pearl," she says.

Without thinking, I wave.

"Can I play?" she asks. Nadine and Ce-Ce take one look at her and turn their backs.

"Sure," I say, despite the hint from Nadine and Ce-Ce; then I throw my jacket on the ground because I've gotten hot. "We could use another player." Gee joins my team. But she is all thumbs and has two left feet. She can't catch or kick or run.

Nadine and Ce-Ce get a few runs off of her in no time. When we are ahead of them again, Nadine tags me out awfully hard. Harder than she needs to. It stings my arm.

Then Nadine and Ce-Ce keep getting the score wrong, and when I tell them what it is, Nadine pushes me. "Liar," she says.

"I'm not lying."

"You're a liar and a tattletale, you scrawny-butted

236

know-it-all." I can't believe the way she's treating me until Ce-Ce underscores the remarks by hitting me with the ball.

"Yeah, why don't you go on back home to your mama," Ce-Ce says.

"Or better yet, to your raggedy friend who got us in trouble. My grandma almost whupped the living daylights out of me," Nadine snaps, saying all of this while shaking her hips at me like they are loaded guns.

"Yeah," Ce-Ce says. "I wish I had been there. I would have straightened you out."

I look at Gee, who is backing away. I want to tell her that none of this is true. That I'm not the one who started the trouble that night. That I didn't hit Artemesia. That everybody was responsible for knocking over Mrs. Mumby's pots and vases.

Then Dink starts jumping up in people's faces again. "There's gonna be a fight! There's gonna be a fight!" he says.

"And take your fat friend with you," Nadine says, looking at Gee.

"What did you say?" Gee asks.

"You heard me, roly-poly," Nadine says.

"I ain't hardly scared of you two midgets."

"Nadine," Ce-Ce says, "she called you a midget."

Nadine reaches over and starts shoving Gee. Soon they are both pushing and punching her. A big girl like Gee. She is twice as big as them.

"Come on, Gee," Dink says. "Sit on them like you do me." Suddenly, Gee doesn't look like the tough heavyweight boxer who I first met. She looks scared. But why are they picking on her? They don't even know her. I don't need to be down here. I have more fun things to do at home. Then just as soon as I turn to go, Gee falls down and Nadine kicks her.

"Leave her alone," I say. The words come out without my knowing it, like when you are at the movies rooting for the good guys and you find yourself talking out loud.

"Say what?" Nadine says, whipping around.

"I said: Leave her alone."

"I got some of this for you too," Nadine says.

"Really?"

"Yeah, you two-faced creep. I told Lenore you were nothing."

"Really?"

Then before I know it, Ce-Ce has slipped behind me and grabbed my arms. Nadine begins punching and kicking me. I am scared. I have never been in a fight before. Everybody crowds around. I am crying and struggling and trying to wriggle free.

I have sharp pains in my sides and in my legs where Nadine's shoes dig into me. I yelp with each blow and double over. Then I am mad. Mad because I am scared and crying. Because they are cheating. Because they are calling me and Gee names. Because I followed them before and watched them beat up Artemesia and didn't say anything. And it wasn't fair. After all those weeks of feeling bad about Artemesia, I just snap. They don't know who they're messing with.

I kick Nadine in the stomach and buck Ce-Ce off my arms, knocking them both down. Then I run and jump on Nadine, and lo and behold, Gee gets up and jumps on Ce-Ce.

"Get off me, you fat pig," Ce-Ce yells.

"Ahh, you got her now, Gee!" I hear Dink say.

I punch Nadine and twist her arm, and say, "Now, you listen to me. You are not going to bully me this time." She is fighting to get my hand loose, scratching and trying to bite me. "You are going to tell Gee that you are sorry."

"Never!" Nadine yells, and spits in my face. I twist harder.

"Owww!" she yells.

"Say you are sorry!" I twist more. I hear her yelp.

"Let go of my arm! Let go! Owww! You breaking my arm. . . . I'm sorry!" she says finally.

Then I get up. Ce-Ce is still flailing under Gee like a squashed bug. There seems to be more to say. To straighten things out, to clear the air. I do not expect Nadine or Ce-Ce to say anything decent. They have stooped pretty low. But I am burning inside, not because of Nadine or Ce-Ce, but because of myself.

"I was too much of a coward to say it before, but I'll say it now. I'm sorry, Artemesia. I know you aren't here to hear this. But I'm sorry that I didn't speak up for you. Sorry that I wasn't a better friend. A real friend."

Then I start for home.

26

TRUTH BE TOLD

Gee follows me, with Dink on her heels. We tell Mama all about what happened. How I got the scratch on my face. Gee talks about how I saved her life.

But fighting isn't for me. The next day Nadine and Ce-Ce—who I have played with all year, who I hit and kicked yesterday as hard as I could—apologize to me.

They stand on the front porch—Ce-Ce with her mother and Nadine with her grandmother—and tell me that they are sorry. Nadine says she did it because she was angry for getting in trouble the night of the basketball game, for being called "a bad influence" by Lenore's mother.

I lean against my mother in the front doorway and look at them. "It's okay," I say. I know that coming to someone's house with your parents is hard. I know that saying you are wrong is hard. I know that trying to right a mistake is hard.

Nadine cries the hardest.

When they are through, they turn and leave.

It isn't half an hour later when Gee shows up. With her schoolbooks. "Good, I'm glad you're home," she says, standing on the front porch. "Want to do homework together?"

While I am mulling it over, Gee just comes right on in and makes herself comfortable. And talks and talks. "Sometimes kids make fun of me because I'm . . . you know, kind of heavy. But my mother says it's just baby fat and that I'm going to be tall." And, "I knew I was going to like you because you aren't anything like what Dink said." Then she giggles. "You know, that boy Harold is like a puppy in love. Not a real smart puppy, but he stares at you all the time on the playground."

"Throwing an eraser at you is a sign of love?" I ask, telling her about a class incident from last year.

"Girl, some boys are like cavemen. They don't know what to do. You tell them you like flowers, and they drag a tree into your yard." We discuss this. "But that doesn't mean that you have to pay any attention to them. We have plenty of time for boys. Me, I want to be a singer."

When we get around to homework, I help her with math and science and she helps me with social studies and Spanish.

As she's leaving she says, "You *are* going to try out for the glee club, aren't you?"

ICING ON THE CAKE

Tomorrow's my birthday. Twelve. Only one more year until I'm officially a teen.

Mama asks me if there is anyone I want to invite over to have cake and ice cream. I immediately think about the night of the school concert when it was Artemesia's birthday and how we celebrated it without even knowing. *If Artemesia could come, I would invite her,* I think. But she isn't here.

"No," I say weakly.

"Are you sure?"

"Yes," I say.

Although it is a Saturday, I spend most of my birthday working on a school project in my room. Everybody else is running around—errands, clean-ing—and I know what they are up to when I smell the unmistakable sweet aroma of cake baking. It isn't in plain sight when I come down for dinner, so I'm expecting a surprise.

We are clearing away the dinner dishes when the doorbell rings.

"I'll get it!" Diana calls, rushing to the front

hallway. I figure it is one of her friends coming by. So I stay in the kitchen scraping table scraps, piling up the dishes and pots and pans to be washed, and wiping up the kitchen counters.

Then Mama calls me from the dining room. "Pearl, can you come in here?"

"Just a minute," I say. I wipe my hands on the dishtowel, and when I go back into the dining room, people yell: "*Sur-priiise!*" My whole family is sitting around the dining-room table, plus Gee and Mrs. Mumby. There, in the center of the table, is a frosted cake decorated with flowers and birds and twelve candles burning, along with gift-wrapped packages.

They start singing "Happy Birthday," with Gee singing the loudest and the best. Gosh, she sounds just like Diana Ross with the Supremes. I blow out the candles and make a wish.

We haven't even gotten to eating the dessert yet when Angela starts jumping up and down, insisting that I begin opening presents. I open hers first. It is lavender-scented bubble bath. I get a slip and my very first pair of nylons—the new panty hose that you don't need a garter belt for. I've been wanting to try those. Curtis gives me a poster with the moon and the planets of the solar system on it.

Gee gives me some stationery decorated with hearts and flowers. And Mrs. Mumby gives me a framed picture. When I tear the paper off, I see right away that it is one of Artemesia's works. Two girls sharing an ice-cream cone.

I will keep this picture my whole life. And I will find Artemesia. For the first time in my life, I know what it is like to be so happy that you cry. Tears stream down my face, though I am smiling. I hug everybody and thank them. Angela, Diana, Mrs. Mumby. . . . And when I hug Gee, she is crying too. And she says, "You're the best friend I ever had."

And I know she means it. A friend likes you even if your nose *is* running from crying. Even if you look different. Or if you are big-boned or bird-legged or the color of silky night. A friend sees what is in your heart.

about the author

Marie Bradby's first book for young readers was the IRA Award–winning *More Than Anything Else*, illustrated by Chris K. Soentpiet. They also collaborated on *Momma, Where Are You From?*, a Golden Kite Honor Book. Growing up in the Washington, D.C., area in the 1960s, Ms. Bradby was a young girl during the Civil Rights movement and the great years of the Motown sound.

She lives with her husband and teenage son in Louisville, Kentucky.